Distinct Desire

C. R. McBride

Part Three of 'The Coffee Café' Series

If you would like more information on any of my books please take a look at my website www.crmcbride.co.uk where you can subscribe to receive up to date information on any of my books and be the first to know release dates and read any teasers.

You can also follow me on Twitter or on Facebook all links are on my website.

Thank you

Other Titles by C.R McBride

Bitter Reflections
Part 1 of The Coffee Café Series

Absolute Resolve
Part 2 of The Coffee Café

About The Coffee Café Series.

The Coffee Café is a place where friends are made, lovers meet and relationships begin. Of course how they will end is yet to be known...

Happy reading xx

Chapter 1

TJ WAS SITTING IN THE CORNER booth of The Coffee Café, like she had done a hundred times before; this was her seat, her little tradition. Carla and TJ met every Friday without fail for coffee to catch up and gossip about the directions their lives were taking. It was a regular hang out for them, full of atmosphere and noise, more like meeting up in a pub than a coffee house.

Today though, the café had lost its sparkle for TJ; sure it was busy, music played in the background and people lounged in the comfy seats, laughing or working at the various tables that filled the café. But today Carla was not there, in truth, she had not been there for over six months, but today hit TJ hard as it was Carla's 21st birthday and she had not been able to send her so much as a card.

She desperately missed her.

Carla had been TJ's best friend ever since they started university together; they had shared classes, worked together on projects and eventually shared a flat together. It had been a fantastic two years and though Carla was quiet and shy, TJ had soon brought her out of her shell, and the pair had had some wild adventures. That was until Carla had met a man over the internet and had fallen head over heels with him. TJ knew they had seen each other several times since then, and that she definitely did not want TJ to meet him yet for fear that she might scare him away. Then one day TJ had received a letter saying that Carla and her new man were leaving town, he had been offered a job abroad and she had decided to leave with him, it had all been last minute and so they had never had the chance to say goodbye.

Carla wrote that she would send TJ a forwarding address as soon as they were settled, and that TJ was her only family, or the only family that cared about her anyway. TJ knew very little of Carla's family, just that they had lost touch years ago and Carla had left as soon as she was old enough. Her best friend never spoke of them or had any contact with them; it made TJ sad for her. But now six months had passed, and Carla had never sent her an address or a card on her birthday, or any sign that she cared. Some family she was!

"You alright, TJ?" the waiter asked as he brought over her third cup of coffee.

"Yeah I'm fine, Mike, how's you?" She knew all the waiters as most of them had been at uni with her. He smiled and they chatted for a while before he returned to his duties and left TJ to continue her coffee.

Things had changed so much, it was scary; she had lost her best friend, left uni and was now about to try and make it in the world. She had completed her course in Photography, Video and Digital Imaging and had built up a huge portfolio of work; her tutors had been more than impressed and selected her to have her work displayed in a local studio. Of course she was delighted at this, it was an unbelievable opportunity but her usual cocky swagger was beginning to dwindle the closer it got to opening night, which was tonight.

Without Carla there to support her she felt lost and alone, and just wished that her friend would contact her; she had secretly hoped that Carla would suddenly burst through the doors at any moment surprising her with a trip home for her birthday... but no visit was made.

"You're not honestly having another, are you?" Mike joked as TJ drained her cup.
"No, that's me done," she replied gloomily.
"Big party to go to, I suppose?" he asked, hinting for an invitation.
"Something like that," TJ muttered and, grabbing her bag, walked out of the busy coffee house.

It was a warm summer day as she strolled home, even slower than usual, dragging her already ripped shoes on the pavement. She stopped to watch two dogs frolicking about in the park as their owners sat on a bench chatting away; they jumped and pranced around each other as though they were dancing. TJ fought the urge to reach into her bag to retrieve her camera and stay a while, absorbed in the dogs' play, but she had to get back, had to get ready for the big event.

The dogs bounded over to her as she walked past.

"Oh, I'm so sorry," the owner called out. "Sam, get down now." The two dogs leapt up at her and nearly knocked her over, but TJ didn't care, she longed for a dog of her own.

"It's fine," she reassured the owner and began to fuss the dog as he licked her arm and hands. She turned her attention to the other dog, who happily wagged his tail vigorously as TJ scratched his ears. "Sorry, boys, I have to go," she announced and giving them one last scratch, resumed her journey home.

"Leaving it a little late, aren't we?" Her flatmate, Suzy, reprimanded as TJ strolled in throwing her bag onto the table and launching herself with a sigh onto the sofa.

Suzy had moved in a few months ago, she was studying Art and Design and been looking for a flat to share and had asked if she could move in when Carla moved out suddenly. TJ shivered as she remembered coming home to find all Carla's clothes gone, all her belongings just taken whilst TJ was at an interview, a short letter sent a day later saying she had gone. Her heart ached for her friend, her laugh and sense of humour had always cheered TJ up no matter what happened. Now, she was alone and she felt betrayed and angry at Carla. TJ was happy that her friend had found love, she was happy that Carla had started a new exciting life. But to forget her best friend altogether, to never attempt to stay in touch, hurt TJ so much.

"You okay?" Suzy walked around the sofa to sit with TJ, seeing the sad expression on her face. She was a skinny girl, hardly any meat on her bones and she wore long baggy clothes that swirled around her. She was a total contrast to TJ, who was a lot shorter, very curvy and wore only jeans and vests.
"I'm fine, don't worry, just nervous about tonight, and I miss Carla, it's her twenty-first today and I still haven't heard a word from her. Just upset, that's all!"
Suzy smiled a sympathetic smile. "If she can't be bothered calling her best friend on her birthday then she can't have been your best friend! Good riddance, that's what I say."
TJ nodded in agreement, it still stung though.

Resigned to the fact she had to get ready, she stood up and gave Suzy, a friendly hug that lasted longer than it should; she was right, TJ had to move on.

Glancing around her room she realised it was a sea of photos of Carla, the two of them at parties, at the café, or just messing around. So many happy memories, so many good times, she couldn't understand why Carla had cut her off from her life, she missed her so much. There were few people TJ could call friends, but Carla had been one of them. She could talk to her about anything, nothing was off limits and Carla was always honest and truthful in return. They had spent many nights drinking wine, talking about boys, course work, music, movies and of course, sex. They had such a close bond, TJ could never understand what had happened to make her leave and just forget about her.

One by one she began to unpin all the photographs and place them in her top drawer, locking away all the pain she felt as she removed her friend from the wall. Trying to control her tears, she gradually removed Carla from her life. All the happy memories were tainted.

Each photo began to annoy her more and more and she violently ripped the last few down, throwing them into the rubbish bin. Gasping for breath between her sobs, she now stood staring at the blank wall before her, all trace of the last few years removed and destroyed.

They were just lies.

TJ stripped off her clothes and stepped under the warm stream of water flowing from her shower; it was heavenly, washing away the tears that had dried on her cheeks as she cleansed her room of Carla.

She washed her hair with her favourite strawberry-scented shampoo and drying herself off, stepped into her bedroom only to hear the over-excited voices of her parents coming from the lounge.

"Good grief, Tabitha, come on, you're going to be late for your own gallery opening!" TJ's mother swung the bedroom door open causing her to grab her towel to hide her modesty.

"Mother! I'm not dressed in here, close the door!" she cried out, mortified.

Her mother just shook her head in amusement.

"Your father isn't bothered and neither am I; now for goodness sake get ready." She began to fuss around inspecting the clothes TJ had hung over the wardrobe door ready to wear. She had chosen a plain, black, knee-length dress, a safe option, she thought. Her mother, in comparison, wore a bright blue dress with peacocks all over it, her Greek style gold sandals peeking out from underneath.

TJ's mother and father were a little...eccentric, they believed children should grow freely and so TJ had never been scolded or disciplined as a child. She was wild to say the least, it was only when her frustrated teachers took her to one side and tried to calm her that she eventually started to take school seriously and worked hard to get a place at university. They had offered extra lessons and interesting projects, and rewarded her when she behaved appropriately. Shocked by the girl's outrageous behaviour and temper they had tried every trick in the book to turn this wild, erratic child into a focused, studious young woman. They had succeeded in the most part, but TJ's temper was still an issue that only she could deal with.

June and Geoffrey, her parents, were the epitome of modern hippies; they wore outrageously bright, flowery clothes and found everything 'amazing' and 'awesome'. They never argued, never had as much as a cross word and whilst everyone thought them a little weird, they were liked.

TJ was nothing like them, she had a temper so vile she would scream the house down as a toddler, to get her own way, and had not changed much over the years. Whilst she managed to hold conversations now, her temper was never hidden away for long. Her teachers had sent her to anger management classes in an attempt to calm her, long enough to allow them to get through a class without interruption, but she had proven to be too much for even them. All she had gained from weeks and weeks of meetings and observations of her, were a few calming techniques and a yoga DVD.

It was not TJ's style to be nervous, she usually had an air of confidence about most things that she did, but having her work on display in the gallery was definitely unnerving. She dressed and put on her makeup, trying to overcome the nausea that was brewing in her stomach and threatening to show itself.

"Here, sweetie, try this." Her mother arrived with a glass of water.

"What's this for?" TJ asked.

"For the nerves, I have some tablets if you feel a little dizzy."

"I am NOT nervous, Mother!" TJ hissed, "And I certainly don't need any tablets to calm me down. I am absolutely fine."

Her voice grew louder and louder, her hands beginning to clench in frustration. Her mother just slowly lifted her eyes, tilting her head to the side and gave TJ a warning stare. June usually walked out of the room when TJ blew her top, refusing to return until she was calm again. Her temper was an expression of her feelings; whilst she encouraged TJ to express herself, that didn't mean she had to be there in the blast zone.

TJ needed her tonight, she needed the protection her parents gave her whilst people ogled her work, commenting or criticising. The last thing she needed was her mother walking out and her father following like a little puppy dog.

"I'm sorry," she managed to mutter; her mother smiled in triumph and handed TJ the water, which she sipped slowly this time.

"Your father and I are very proud of you, sweetie."

"I know, Mum, thanks, I just..." TJ did not need to finish her apology, her mother had her wrapped up in a warm and loving embrace before she could finish. She returned the hug sighing deeply, inhaling the gentle vanilla smell of her mother's face cream. They had such a close bond despite TJ's battles, she loved her family with every ounce of her body and, as she was an only child, they doted on her in return.

"Come on, let's get you ready," her mother encouraged, unzipping the dress for TJ, to step into and then zipping her up, brushing her hair away from her shoulders. "Are you wearing your hair up or down?" she asked. Staring into the mirror, she pulled all TJ's long blonde hair into a ponytail, twisted it and then placed it at the back of her head in a loose bun. Then allowed it to cascade down again, brushing half forward to trail over one shoulder. "I like it down; it falls so beautifully all loose."

"I actually wanted to pull it back tonight, Mum, kind of professional," she admitted, not wanting to offend her. Brushing it into a sleek wet ponytail, she fastened it back.

"Good decision, dear," her mother agreed. "Put a spare band on your arm, in case that one breaks then," she suggested.

It made TJ smile as she remembered the endless supply of elastic bands she used to go through when it was suggested she use them as a distraction, when she felt her temper raging. She would pull the band so hard it would snap straight off causing a stinging, red line to appear across her wrist. The spare hairband would serve as a substitute if tonight got too much for her, which she was sure it would do.

Why on earth she had agreed to this was beyond her.

Her father chatted away happily in the car, but TJ was barely listening as she fought the churning that was happening in her stomach. Her defences turned her nervousness into anger and she began to get cross with herself for feeling this way. Her mother turned around in her seat, watching her daughter closely.

"If you need to scream, honey, just let it out," she told her.

"For God's sake, Mother! I am fine - KNOCK. IT. OFF!" Her mother just smiled and returned to gazing forward out of the windscreen. "Mum, I'm..." TJ began, but immediately her mother cut her off again. "Do not apologise for who you are, TJ, you are young and passionate, that is not a thing to say sorry for."

TJ grinned; just once it might be nice to have her mother or father chastise her about the way she spoke to them, just once she would like to feel guilty about losing her temper, but they were who they were and saw nothing wrong with their daughter expressing her emotions as and when she needed to.

Turning into the gallery car park, TJ's father gave a childish chuckle. "It's exciting isn't it, I mean, that's our little girl's work that people are paying to come and see." He squeezed his wife's hand, tightly leaning in to kiss her.

"Please don't start that now," TJ begged. "Please, I will walk if you two start making out in the car or especially in there!" she warned. As much as she enjoyed being in a loving family and having her parents be so happy and in love after years together, she could not deal with their overly friendly, public displays of affection. Her parents just laughed at her and continued their kiss.

"Right, I am out of here." TJ opened the car door and got out, closely followed by her parents. Again the nerves appeared as she came face to face with a sign outside the front of the gallery:

Special exhibition
By TJ Knapley.
This week only.
Special opening tonight 7pm.

TJ sucked in a breath, her work was good, she knew that, her teachers had praised her photographs and set this up. They wouldn't have done that if they had any doubts, she knew this, so why was her stomach swirling around and around? Her mother slid her hand into her daughter's and her father appeared on the other, mirroring his wife's actions.

At that moment she was five years old again on her first day of school, supported by her loving parents who practically dragged her into class that first day. She wasn't five anymore but the confidence began to fill her again and her balance and posture returned. She lifted her head high.

"Right, come on, let's do this," she chanted and walked towards the gallery ready to face her critics.

Chapter 2

THE GALLERY WAS NOT EMPTY as she had anticipated, but in contrast it was filled with people; a hum of hushed voices greeted her as she entered. The gallery owner was waiting for her, a tall thin woman with glasses perched on the end of her nose.

"TJ, I am so glad you are here, what a fantastic turn out. You have already had a number of people interested in purchasing your work," she fussed excitedly.

"Buy them?!! I didn't realise they were for sale here, I thought they were just for exhibition." Her mouth hung open and her head began to spin at the thought that someone might actually want to have her work displayed on their wall.

"They weren't, but honestly we should think about some prices because people are LOVING them, and of course the gallery would take a percentage," she grinned slyly. "Go and talk to that lady over there, she is our curator and she will give you an idea of what prices people might be willing to pay tonight, we can help you price up if you decide to continue to sell through us."

TJ stood flabbergasted at her words, she had not prepared herself for this at all and her parents just grinned like little kids at the circus. Leaving them to get a drink, TJ took her first good look at the exhibition; she had been here a number of times to arrange the work and talk about how it would look when displayed, but somehow, with different lighting and all the people, it was not the same, it had taken on a whole new ambiance, a life of its own.

Her work was divided into separate sections, The Environment, Home Life, Questions and Truth, each display area having its own lighting and atmosphere. She found herself lost as she walked around each area; her pictures enlarged and framed in large gold, elaborate mouldings, all hanging on a stark red brick wall.

There were photos of her favourite childhood places, the river, the endless fields around her parents' house, first with all wild flowers in full bloom and then, deeply covered in snow, equally beautiful. She smiled as she saw the pictures of her parents and the ridiculous objects scattered around their shambles of a home, so many happy memories. An endless pile of inanimate, unwanted, useless possessions all carefully placed, all belonging exactly where they were. They loved the extraordinary.

She sighed as she walked towards the painful pictures of mistreated animals and children that she had taken last year as part of her coursework.

"TJ, come and meet some people," the gallery owner called out to her, dragging her away from a particularly emotional image she had taken of a child surrounded by toys and presents. The child was curled up in a foetal position crying. Her mother had shed tears when she saw that photograph. TJ had meant it as a show of materialism, but her mother saw a child's heart that had all it wanted but nothing it needed, it was missing love. She had always believed that TJ could see things other people couldn't, she could take a simple photograph but in that picture she would capture every emotion and feeling, even if she couldn't see it or feel it herself.

"Hi, sorry, I am coming." Several people began to whisper to each other as she passed them, just now realising that she was the artist whose work they were admiring.

"TJ, this is Barbara Morgan, she is a good friend of the gallery and has supported many new artists in the past." TJ shook the woman's hand and smiled warmly.

"So what do you think of my work?" she asked. "Do you think it shows promise?"

Barbara stared deeply into her eyes. "You don't really want me to tell you if your work has merit, do you?" she quizzed.

"No, not really," TJ laughed, feeling a warmth towards this woman immediately. "It's just nice to hear other people like them. I, of course, think I am ace!" Barbara roared with laughter, causing everyone to turn and focus on their conversation, but Barbara seemed oblivious to the attention.

"Tell me, do you take on private commissions, TJ?" she began, then added, "I feel a bit strange calling you TJ, does it stand for a real name?"

It was now TJ's turn to laugh.

"Yeah, I'm not really keen on my name so just shorten it to TJ, it's Tabitha." Her eyes rolled around to focus on anything but the woman's face.

"And the J?" Barbara continued relentlessly.

"Jemima," TJ all but whispered.

"I see," Barbara stated sympathetically. "Not really a lot you can do with those names, is there." She stifled a little chuckle. "No offence to your parents of course, it's just that they're not your traditional sort of names, are they? How about Jem?" she offered.

"Just when it is us talking, so I don't feel like a teenager." TJ agreed, Jem sounded quite grown up.

"I have never been asked to do any work, I mean I have just left uni so I do need a job but I don't know where I want to go yet." Her face screwed up as she faced her blank future prospects. She had no idea what she wanted to do. The idea of doing the same thing day in and day out petrified her. She wanted to do lots of different projects, things that would stretch and challenge her.

"Would you like to meet me for lunch tomorrow?" Barbara asked. "I may have a project for you, if you are interested?" She handed TJ a business card, which she accepted greedily and promised to call her to make arrangements. The gallery owner smiled and moved TJ on to meet other people who were hovering around the group, anxiously waiting their turn to meet her.

It was a strange mix of people at the exhibition, rich people, businessmen and women, fellow art students or graduates, each one complimenting her on her work. It was surreal as she made her way around the room thanking people for coming and for their kind words. Her parents had taken great delight in standing near the pictures of themselves and explaining to everyone the history behind the weird and wonderful objects in the pictures.

"They are the best marketing tool I have ever seen!" the gallery owner had joked. "Can I keep them here for the week and just have them stand there talking?"

"You can keep them permanently, they are off their rockers," TJ replied affectionately.

She talked to various people there about her work, her inspirations and where she found the locations for her photographs. Her perceptions of an image could change when viewed at different angles and so she never liked to take photos straight on, but rather would climb into awkward positions to get the right shot. Of course, this had resulted in numerous falls and broken bones and ruined clothes but hey ho, an artist was supposed to suffer for their art.

By the end of the evening, TJ's head was buzzing from the numerous glasses of champagne and the endless stream of people she had met who had showered her with positive feedback and praise. It had been the most amazing night of her life. She had been given a handful of business cards from people all wanting to talk about opportunities for her, and wanting to commission work. Her parents had both had their fill of alcohol and were one drink away from breaking into song and telling stories about her childhood.

"Maybe we should get a taxi home, eh?" she suggested, taking the car keys from her father's hands and placing them firmly into her mother's handbag. Her usually quiet father was engaged in a heated discussion with a few of the stragglers, and now interrupted his discussion to wave his fists in the air.

"No," he slurred. "I drive myself, thank you."

Her mother just laughed at him.

"I called one ten minutes ago, darling. Don't worry, we will get home fine, promise you will call me tomorrow?"

TJ promised and tried, along with the gallery owner, to bustle her father out of the exhibition and into a taxi cab.

"Is it okay to leave my dad's car here?" she asked.

"Of course, of course, anything for my new find," the owner winked. "You made some fantastic sales tonight, you know, I think you may have sold the majority of your work by the end of the week."

TJ frowned, she had discussed prices with the curator but hadn't in a million years thought people would pay them. "I think that by the end of the week you can kiss your uni fees goodbye," she added.

"You are kidding!" TJ spat the remains of her champagne all over the floor but the gallery owner just nodded, knowingly.

"Your work is just the right combination, TJ, you have a unique view of the world but it is still beautiful and something that people want to have on their walls. I think you will get a lot of work from this. I will expect you to remember me when you are a famous artist or doing cover shoots for top magazines or doing whatever it is that you want to do!"

TJ was overwhelmed; this evening had gone from a little ego boost exercise, to pushing her out into the world as a serious professional. "Come on, let's get you in your taxi, you be okay getting home?" TJ nodded silently, stunned at the difference one night had made to her life.

As the taxi pulled up outside her flat, Suzy rushed out to meet her. "Hey how did it go? Did everyone like them? Well, of course they did, I mean it's you, right. I mean were you happy? Did you enjoy yourself?"

TJ just smiled, paid the taxi driver and walked into her flat.

"Come on, TJ, you are killing me, tell me everything!" She was practically jumping up and down in excitement. Her shift at the dress shop she worked in had meant she couldn't go to the opening but TJ had shown her around the exhibition already and she intended to go again during the week.

TJ held her hands up to calm Suzy down. "It went well, really well, really, really, really well!" The excitement began to build up in her again.

"Oh my God, I knew it," Suzy squealed.

"I also sold a few." At this Suzy screeched so loudly that TJ had to cover her ears. "I know. The gallery thinks I may make enough to pay off all my student loans by the end of the week."

The realisation of this was slowly sinking in, no more panicking about debts, no more worrying and being forced into taking jobs she didn't want to. Tears began to fall and she hastily wiped them away, not really knowing why they were falling, Suzy lunged forward, wrapping her arms tightly around her friend...

"I am so happy for you, TJ." She joined her in the tearful hug. "I mean I am not surprised, I told you your work is amazing, but I am so happy."

"Hey, I almost forgot," TJ began, changing the subject slightly. "This guy asked me for your number, he loved the photographs I took of some of your dresses and he said that he loved the designs." She dug around into her bag and pulled out a card, Suzy gawped at her, stunned.

Suzy had made some unbelievably beautiful and intricate dresses and clothes for her course. Naturally, TJ was always used as the model for them and spent many hours in outfits with painful pins digging into her. So when she had been instructed to take photos of home life she had taken pictures of Suzy working on her dresses at a mannequin, or the dresses on a washing line, blowing in a breeze.

The man had said he had never seen such delicate designs on unusual fabrics and asked for Suzy's details. It was now Suzy's turn to be excited and she hugged the card to her chest gratefully. It was TJ's night to advertise her own work and here she was talking about her friend's talent, she was such a generous person.

Not everyone 'got' TJ, she could seem brash and offish at times, but once you got to know her you realised that she would never deliberately cause offence or harm to anyone. She just had a crap way of dealing with things. But right at this moment,

Suzy had never been more proud to call TJ her friend.

As the two girls chatted, fatigue suddenly caught up with them and TJ felt her eyelids drooping. "I need to go to bed," she announced, Suzy agreeing with her.
"Thank you," Suzy said. "For the card, and the flat and everything you do. I know you miss Carla, but I do appreciate you and I would never leave without staying in touch, I promise."
"Thanks, Suze, I know you wouldn't. I do love ya," she offered playfully, Suzy punched her arm and went off to her room.

TJ picked her bag up and dragged herself to her own room, too tired to get a shower; she slipped on her old baggy T-shirt and climbed into bed. She was exhausted; the emotions of the day had been draining, but she had worried for nothing, people had loved her work and now she had a lunch date that may lead to a job.

Looking up at the pale blue ceiling she smiled to herself; in just one night, she had gone from a student, to a working professional, with an income to prove it. She giggled out loud, still not believing that people had actually bought her work, actually paid money.

As she snuggled down under the covers, sleep finally took over and as her heavy eyelids closed, she felt exhilarated for what tomorrow may bring, and for the first time in months she slept without thinking of her absent best friend.

Chapter 3

THE ALARM CLOCK FELT like a drill burying its way into TJ's skull when it rang out the next morning. It was now clear to her that she was NOT a champagne drinker. The searing pain was no small side effect and the little buzz she had received the night before was not worth feeling the horrendous pounding she felt now.

She thumped her hand repeatedly on the snooze button to shut the damn thing off, then rolled onto her back trying to focus. Every movement resulted in her stomach churning, threatening to evacuate the liquid poison, but lying still was causing the room to spin wildly out of control. A sweat began to build; the surface of her skin began to boil whilst at the same time causing shivers and goose bumps to appear through the wet clammy skin. There was no escaping it, she knew what needed to be done and throwing back the covers she rushed into the bathroom, barely making it before her retching stomach finally won its battle.

"You alive, babe?" Suzy exclaimed, after TJ had not emerged after fifteen minutes. TJ sat staring at the blank bathroom wall; slowly she began to come around, her stomach now settling after it had removed its entire contents, the room now still, allowing her to focus on one spot. She gingerly got to her feet and opened the door.

"Holy shit, TJ, what the hell were you drinking?" Suzy cried out, seeing the state of her friend who was shuffling across the floor, her hair plastered to her, what can only be described as, green face.

"Champagne," TJ whimpered, her puppy dog eyes pleading with Suze to make it go away, her lip jutting out regretfully.

"Oh crap - you need bacon butties, my friend." Suzy immediately began banging around in the kitchen, causing TJ to cradle her head.

"Suze, I appreciate it, really I do, but there is no way I can face food right now."

"Trust me, honey, I know what you need. Now sit." She pulled out a chair and placed a pint of orange juice in front of her with some headache tablets. TJ just stared, her whole body ached, why did everything ache?

"I am never drinking again."

"Yeah, whatever."

"I mean it."

"Of course you do, I believe you."

"I am never drinking champagne again, that is for sure." Suzy just laughed.

Oddly enough the orange juice, tablets and bacon butties seemed to bring TJ back to life, her stomach accepted the food and slowly but surely the thumping in her brain eased.

"Thanks, mate. You saved my life," she offered, gratefully gobbling down her third bacon sandwich.

She contemplated going back to bed but remembered she had a lunchtime meeting with the woman from the gallery who had offered her some work. That sounded so funny, a lunchtime meeting, she felt grown up all of a sudden. "I need to get a shower and get ready," she announced.

"Not before a cup of tea," Suzy corrected, and began to make a huge mug.

Suzy fussed around her like a mother hen, it was nice, maybe TJ could let her in a little more. It was obvious that Carla was off living her life, not giving her friend a second thought. TJ always worried about letting someone else in, allowing herself to become close to someone that could hurt her. But Suzy was a lovely person, she cared a lot about TJ and had a huge circle of friends of her own, and didn't need a new best friend, maybe it would be okay to get a little closer; maybe.

The warm water cascading from the shower flowed over her skin, washing away all the toxins and bad feelings she had experienced; she stood with her hands bracing herself against the wall, just letting the stream wash away all the toxins from her body, it was bliss.

She reached out for her usual pampering products and began scrubbing away at her skin until she felt all new and refreshed; the hangover became just a memory as the life-giving water renewed her. She was consumed with how today would play out, would this be a doorway to a career? Could this woman really offer her a job? Reluctantly she turned off the heavenly water and stepped out of the shower, scrubbing herself dry until she was pink and raw. Today called for a bit of luxury, she needed a bit of pampering to perk herself up. She selected an oil for her skin to ease the itching that was created by over-scrubbing; now she needed to treat the new fresh skin that had been exposed. The smooth, warm liquid glided over her curves and TJ began to feel herself tingle, her breath shortening at the feel of her own touch. Maybe she could spare ten minutes, just to please herself, allow herself to be fully relaxed before the meeting.

Suzy called out that she was leaving just as TJ left her bedroom; the glare Suzy gave her was stern.
"Are you really going to that meeting in jeans?"
"Yes."
"Really?"
"YES."
"Really, really?"

"Suzy, sod off to work." Suzy shrugged her shoulders and slammed the door deliberately, but TJ was unaffected now after her re-birthing ritual.

TJ always wore jeans, it was her signature outfit, she never wore dresses or skirts unless it was a formal do like last night. Her daily attire was jeans, vest or t-shirt and jacket, not forgetting the camera bag that was constantly thrown over her shoulder. How could you go climbing in a skirt? What if there was an amazing scene just waiting to be captured but she needed to wade through a field of nettles or through a waterlogged field? No, skirts were not for her.

She drank the tea that Suzy had made and collected her things together. She made the decision to neglect to pack her portfolio as Barbara, the woman she was meeting, had seen most of her work at the gallery opening; instead she opted for a few letters of recommendation and a small album of photos. Then draining her cup, she headed back into her bedroom for one last check. Brushing her hair again, she opted to leave it down today; she wanted to be relaxed, for the meeting to be as informal as possible, after all that was how TJ was. No airs and graces for her, she was a 'what you see, is what you get' girl.

The sun shone brightly as she walked into town, TJ loved this time of year, and springtime was warm enough to be outside but not so hot that you felt drained. Everything was starting afresh, just beginning to bloom. Buds covered the trees overhead and bulbs in the ground were beginning to show, the grass-covered gardens were at their greenest with no brown dry patches to be seen. Everywhere her eyes fell, she could see possibilities.

Barbara had asked to meet her in a small café on the high street. It was not somewhere TJ frequented often, favouring The Coffee Café's more relaxed atmosphere, but it was a nice place and not too formal. Standing outside, TJ suddenly found herself rooted to the spot, again the stomach churning began. What was wrong with her lately? TJ never had a confidence problem before, but over the last few months everything seemed to panic her.

"My son used to have three on his wrist, you know."
A voice from behind caused TJ to spin on the spot and come face to face with Barbara.
"I'm sorry?"
"The bands that you have been playing with for the last five minutes, he had three of them on a bad day. Do you find they work? I failed to see any improvement with Adam, my boy; he just got more annoyed because it hurt!" She chuckled lightly, immediately putting TJ at ease.
"I think it is supposed to be a distraction, stops us breaking things." She laughed then suddenly realised what she had admitted to, but Barbara was just nodding in agreement.
"Yes, I suppose, I took to bubble wrapping everything valuable and putting it into storage when

Adam was young, not that we had much in way of value back then, but personally precious."

TJ knew exactly what she had meant; she had had a massive temper tantrum once and inadvertently smashed her favourite bottle. It was an old fashioned medicine bottle that she used to collect, she would have them lined up all along her shelves and the sunlight would throw coloured rainbows everywhere. She had been devastated when she smashed it and would never be able to replace it, so yes, she knew exactly what this lady meant.

"Shall we go inside then, Jem?" The smile on TJ's face spread further, she liked this woman, she had a lovely way about her, a calming nature that reminded her so much of her art teacher in High School. She had invested so much time and energy in TJ, she made her feel worthwhile, and something told her that this woman was going to do the same thing.

"He didn't!" TJ gasped, laughing at the story Barbara was retelling about her husband.
"He did, right there and then. I could have died. I have never been so embarrassed in my life!"

The two women had been sharing stories for over an hour, each one talking about their friends and family, laughing and joking together like they had been friends forever.

"More tea?" the waiter questioned as he came over to the raucous table again. Barbara nodded and he removed the teapot replacing it with a fresh one. TJ immediately began pouring two cups, offering milk and sugar. Barbara sat back, a little smile playing on the corners of her mouth.

"You are nothing like I thought you would be, Jem," she suddenly announced, causing TJ to panic and wonder if she had done something wrong. "You have a bit of a reputation you know; they tell me you have a temper and quite a fierce one at that. Yet all I have seen is a wonderful, polite, entertaining young lady. So tell me, which is the real you?"

She sat back, giving TJ the floor to explain herself. TJ shuffled uncomfortably in her seat.

"Both, I guess," she admitted honestly. "I am a creative person and that makes me passionate, add that to the fact that I have parents that are bonkers, and you get me."

"They are lovely people and you love them to bits, I see that in you, so don't try to kid a kidder." Barbara sniggered, earning her extra brownie points in TJ's eyes. Her parents were odd and it took most people a while to get used to them before they liked them. "You are avoiding the question, young lady."

"Yes, I have a temper, I know that and I do try to deal with it and most of the time I am the person you see here. My problem is extremes. Any emotion that is too far one way or the other sets me off, nerves, worry, inability to do what I want to do and sometimes, even happiness causes me to lose my rag. I don't feel the need to apologise for it."

Barbara stared intensely at her. "I am not asking you to apologise, my dear, I am just asking."

"It's just an emotion, if you piss me off I will lose it and you will know about it."

Barbara let out a loud booming laugh, causing the entire café to stare at her. Again she showed no remorse, felt no need to apologise, she just laughed, never taking her eyes off TJ.

"Did I say something funny?" TJ asked, not completely understanding what was causing this hysteria. Barbara took her napkin and dabbed her eyes that were now streaming with tears.

"I am sorry, dear. I am not laughing at something you said, I am laughing at something I am about to say, to offer you. I am laughing because... well... it is definitely going to be interesting."

Chapter 4

TJ SAT BACK IN HER CHAIR sucking in her breath, exhaling it loudly and slowly as she deliberated Barbara's proposal. The woman had explained exactly what she wanted TJ to do, and that she would be more than happy to pay well for it.

"Jem, darling, I am not asking anything inappropriate of you; I just want some pictures of my son, that's all."

"Barbara, you are asking me to stay in a house with a man, I do not know, for three or four days, taking pictures of him and hoping to God he doesn't get pissed off with me!" Barbara chuckled at this comment.

"Oh, he will get pissed at you, sweetie, believe me. Something tells me that you will be able to handle it, this is why I am asking you and no one else."

Barbara had only one son, a successful businessman who had taken himself from poor beginnings and turned his life around. He was a self-made man and a fiercely private one. She explained that the company managers had advised him to have some publicity photos taken; the company needed a face not just a logo. It had taken a while but he had finally succumbed to their pleas on the strict understanding that it would not turn into a circus ring. Barbara, however, had her own plans upon hearing him concede, she wanted some personal shots. Photographs that she could hang on her wall, that reflected the carefree boy he used to be, before all the hard work. The man he was when he was at home with his family and no one from the business world was around.

"Please do not misunderstand me, Jem," Barbara explained, "I am immensely proud of all of my son's achievements but it has not been an easy road. He has no university degree, no A Levels or qualifications to prove his intellect. He has worked hard and has had to prove his worth at every turn and that has a major effect on a person, on their personality. Adam never laughs anymore, he never messes around and acts....silly. Do you know what I mean?"

She seemed sad and TJ reached across the table and placed a sympathetic hand across Barbara's. She did understand, not for the same reasons, but people saw TJ's parents and then heard about her reputation of being overly passionate about everything, and just wrote her off. Only a few people had ever invested time and effort into getting to know the real TJ, and given her opportunities in life.

It seemed that Barbara was destined to be one of these people and she was not going to let her down.

Paying the bill, Barbara kissed TJ on the cheek followed by an affectionate hug, an embrace that TJ willingly returned. "I'm so glad you have agreed to this, Jem, I am really looking forward to seeing my son through your eyes." There was a wicked glint in her eye that did not go unnoticed by TJ, but she made no retort and followed her out of the café.

"Goodness, that sun is strong now," Barbara exclaimed as she reached into her handbag to retrieve her sunglasses. "Thank you again, dear, and I will see you soon. I will get someone to email you all the details." TJ managed a smile and began to fish around in her own bag for some glasses, the sunshine blinding her.

Thoughts swirled through her mind as she strolled back home, this was a job, a real job with a wage. Sure it was only a few days' work, but it was a doorway, a chance for people to see a productive side of her work, not just the creative stuff. She could do this; she could spend a few days in a strangers house taking photos - that was, after all, what she loved to do.

A loud shout made TJ jump and spin around eyes wide. Suzy was racing up the path after her, her bag flying around as she ran desperately to catch up to TJ.

"Hey," she breathed heavily as she caught up to her, TJ laughed at her puffed red face. "How did it go? I saw you back there and I tried to catch you but you were in a world of your own, did you not hear me shouting?"

"Oh, I am sorry, Suz; my mind is off with the fairies."

"Yeah I got that." Suzy bent double, dragging breaths in an attempt to fill her lungs.

"Come on, let's grab a coffee and I will tell you all about it."

TJ, led her friend into The Coffee Café and ordered two large cappuccinos, extra foam.

"There's a seat there." Suzy began to head towards a seat when TJ stopped her.

"Do you mind if we sit somewhere else?" she asked, staring at the seat that she used to occupy with Carla, as much as she had grown to love Suze she didn't think she was ready to sit there, in those seats with someone else. "It's just I fancy a big squashy seat today," she lied.

Suzy was immediately pacified and headed towards the huge bright, lime green sofa in the back of the room.

"So?"

"I got the job, it pays and it's just easy portrait sort of stuff."

"My arse!" Suzy barked. "You were miles away back there, and that woman was dressed really nicely - I saw her, and I also saw your face when she left. What is going on? Are you prostituting yourself?"

TJ cried out in shock at Suzy's mocking. "Shut up!"

"Come on, I am seriously going to burst if you don't give me some details here!" She squirmed around in her seat excitedly.

"Aright, her son is some hotshot businessman; he needs some photos taken for his business portfolio and marketing stuff. The man behind it all, so they need some professional shots and some showing his more human side. You know, as though he didn't know the pictures were being taken, sort of thing." Suzy nodded. "At the same time, his mother says that she would like some personal photos taken of him, of him relaxing and being playful and silly. She wants photos that she can put up on her wall at home 'cause she doesn't have many of him as a man. She says she has loads from when he was a boy but it sounds like he is a bit of a workaholic and so she doesn't have many of him grown up."

TJ took a long sip of her cappuccino.

"Shit! That's hot." TJ sucked on her lip as the scalding liquid slid down her throat, causing her to catch her breath. Suzy just frowned at her, dismayed, and shook her head.

"For someone that drinks coffee all the time, you would think you would have learnt to let it cool down first!" she chastised.

"Ha ha."

"So who is this guy? Do we know him?"

"Barbara is sending me all the details this afternoon, the contract is over a few days so I have to stay on the premises, so I can be there all the time."

"Hold on a minute - you are staying at his house? This guy we know nothing about - this guy that could be a mass murderer and you are going to live there!" Suzy nearly shot out of her seat.

"It's not like that; there is a guest room with its own entrance and its own lock." She emphasised the 'own lock' part and Suzy seemed to calm down a little.

"So who is he?"

"Adam Morgan."

Suzy's mouth dropped open. "THE Adam Morgan! As in the owner and creator of The Coffee Café - the very place that we are sitting in?" TJ shrugged her shoulders. "The man that now has branches all over the country and is expanding worldwide." Still, TJ remained in the dark as to who this guy was. So, he was a businessman, so what?

Suzy muttered a whole string of curses that TJ neither heard nor wanted to hear as she rummaged around in her overly large bag. She swiped out her laptop and immediately began setting it up and connecting it to the Wi-Fi connection in the café. "Here!" she cried out triumphantly, as she spun the laptop around for TJ to see the few pictures scattered on the screen.

There were not many, Barbara was right, he definitely kept himself to himself. No photos of him leaving nightclubs with women, no scandals reported, not a drop of excitement at all, just a handful of pictures of Café openings, a few charity functions, and several biographies on him, that was it. TJ clicked on one of the photos to enlarge it.

"Wow!"

"I know, that's what I was telling you."

"Jeez, he's really..."

"Hot? Yes, like off the Richter scale."

TJ enlarged the other photographs, all of him in a smart tailored suit, all of them dazzling. She finally clicked on one of the charity function photos.

"Oh my God!" Her mouth went dry as a full photograph of the most beautiful man opened up; he stood casually in a dinner jacket talking to someone, his bow tie impeccably tied, a champagne glass slightly tilted in his hand. The beauty of the picture took TJ's breath away; surely it was a staged press picture, nothing this perfect could happen naturally.

"I told you, blimey, TJ, and you are gonna have to stay in his house and stare at him all day. Jesus, I wish I was you right now."

Suzy's words played on TJ's mind all day, every time she closed her eyes those damned pictures of him appeared, her body reacting to them. This was going to turn out to be one of the worst decisions she had ever made in her entire life. She was going to have to stay professional and stare at this man twenty-four-seven, watch him in his everyday life, learn about him, discover what made him tick, to allow the lens to fully capture him. But she was going to have to remain professional, keep her emotions, and obvious attraction to him locked away.

"Shit!" she cursed aloud, cradling her head in her hands.
"That is not going to help you pack," Suzy called out from her room.

The empty suitcase had remained so for over an hour. True to her word Barbara had emailed all the details, addresses, schedules everything she could possibly need, but somehow TJ was still sitting on the edge of her bed definitely NOT packing.
"Here, do you want to borrow these?" Suzy strolled in carrying two very short, very revealing dresses.
"What the hell would I want those for?" TJ roared "For God's sake, THIS. IS. A. JOB, Suze, nothing else."
"Yeah, that's why you are getting all 'Hulk' on me right now!"

TJ took a deep breath and twanged the elastic bands circling her wrist. Suzy never did bow down to TJ's temper; she knew there was no malice behind it, just her way of dealing with stress. It was a crap way of dealing with it, but that was TJ.
"I'm sorry."
"I know."
"I know you know, Suze, but I am saying it anyway."
Suzy smiled. "I will be fine, TJ, I am only playing ... and jealous as hell." Suzy threw a sly grin TJ's way.

Slowly and surely with Suzy's help the case began to fill, just t-shirts and jeans, wash stuff, a little makeup and all of TJ's camera equipment. That was all she needed and she meant to start as she meant to continue, professionally.

"Right, I think that is you done," Suzy declared as she closed the case up. "All ready for tomorrow, so now it is wine and Chinese - agreed?"

They actually managed to have a very pleasant evening; the Chinese was amazing as always, and TJ and Suzy found themselves lying on the sofa, jeans undone, as always.

"Why do I eat so much?" Suzy complained. "I don't think my jeans will ever fit again."

"It's such a nice feeling though," TJ chimed in. "Fancy a movie?"

Suzy shook her head.

"What about another glass of wine?"

"Definitely not... and neither do you, you have an early start!"

TJ groaned, she had managed to keep her mind preoccupied so she didn't think about it but now it was getting late and there was no avoiding the fact that this was happening. Suzy had assured her it would be fine, that it was a brilliant opportunity and was bound to open lots of doors for her. She was right, TJ knew that, but she wished someone would tell the butterflies in her stomach.

"I am going to clear the kitchen and then head to bed," Suzy announced.

They scraped all the leftovers into a bag and TJ took the rubbish out whilst Suzy washed up. The cool, night air stung her face, quite the opposite to the raging sun from the day, as she made her way to the bins outside their apartment. Thank goodness it was on the ground floor, she couldn't imagine how much of a pain it would be to have to trail down flights of stairs every time she put bins out.

"Hey, beautiful." TJ turned to see a guy following her to the bins.

"Hi," she returned uneasily.

"You live here?"

TJ was already bored with the conversation and just walked past him but he had other ideas and reached to grab her arm.

"Hey, get off," TJ called out but the man just laughed.

"Come on, I am just being friendly." He smiled, presumably she was supposed to melt into his arms at this point and giggle girlishly. That's not exactly what happened next, what did happen is that TJ stamped as hard as she could on his foot followed by a kick to his shin. As he crumpled up into a heap he swore,

"Fucking bitch!"

"What? No more 'hello beautiful' anymore?"

She turned her back on him; what was it with guys like that, take what they want and sod everything else? Instead of going back to the flat she walked over to the caretaker's apartment. He wasn't really a caretaker but he helped students find accommodation near the university and always looked out for them. If anyone needed to know that there was a prick walking around then it was him, he might be able to set up some cameras or lights around the dark rubbish area.

It was late by the time she had retold her story, and Suzy sat next to her having come outside to search for her when she didn't return.
"What a prat!" Suzy exclaimed.
The caretaker agreed and told her he would put up some notices advising the girls to be careful, he would also try talking to the landlords about improving security in that area.
"Be careful, girls, in future, no solo trips, yes?"

The caretaker was a lovely guy, in his late fifties he had taken his duties as a caretaker beyond his job description and had taken it upon himself to make sure all the students had safe, decent living accommodation. Of course, TJ had neglected to tell him that she was now no longer a student and therefore really should be moving out. There was time for that later.

"Right, this time I am definitely off to bed, 'night, TJ."
"'Night, Suze, and thanks for listening to me today."
"That's what I am here for; I expect a quick text followed up by a full email as soon as you get a chance tomorrow. I want to know if Adam Morgan is that beautiful in person!"
"Deal."

Great, TJ thought to herself as she laid her head on her pillow, *now I am going to be thinking about him again*. Maybe dreaming about him, this was going to be a nightmare.

How could she have such a huge crush on someone from just a few photos? But then again she recalled his mother, Barbara, telling her that her son was very cut off and private. Maybe he would be a complete arsehole and TJ would no longer have anything to worry about.

She could but hope.

Chapter 5

TJ's HEART RACED AS the taxi pulled up outside a huge apartment block across town - the posh end of town. Her eye line was raised as she followed the windows all the way to the top; she could only imagine the views from up there.

It had taken her an hour to decide what to wear that morning; jeans seemed too hot for the latest heatwave, but a dress was completely out of the question if the dreams that she had been subjected to through the night were anything to go by. No, she had decided on long shorts, high tops and a plain white vest, very boring, very appropriate.

"Can I help you?" the man sitting behind the desk asked as TJ entered the reception hall of the building.

"Erm, I am here to see Mr Morgan. I'm TJ Knapley."

"Of course, the photographer. Right, I have instructions to give you this key card, this will only open the door to the guest room, which is located to the left of the main apartment. The interlocking door is locked from both sides so if it doesn't open then it is locked from the other side."

TJ nodded, trying to take in all that he was saying.

"I need to see some proof of ID and also I need you to sign here for the key."

TJ took the pen from the man's hand and then searched through her purse for her driving licence. He smiled politely. "Right, there is a list of rules in here, no parties, no pets etc, these are the building regulations and must be adhered to at all times. So all that is left to do is take the lift on your left up to the top floor and Mr Morgan will meet you there to give you the lift codes and such. If you would like to leave your luggage here someone will bring it up to you." He offered his hand and she shook it.

"Erm, thank you but I will take my luggage myself, I appreciate it though."

TJ had no intention of leaving all her camera equipment in the hands of a minimum wage baggage handler. Nice or not, it was all too valuable. She dragged her case to the lift and pressed the highest button, nerves again attacking, causing her to waver a little as the lift rocked her on its ascent. TJ straightened up her hair that was pulled back into a tight ponytail, then smoothed her shorts down, making sure there were no food stains or coffee stains spoiling the desired effect.

"Ms Knapley, a pleasure to meet you." The man that greeted her was most definitely not Adam Morgan, he was short and round, with glasses perched on the tip of his nose. He reached out.

"I have it, thank you," she blurted, reaching for her bag a little too quickly, leaving the man with his hand stretched out in greeting. "Oh, I am so sorry," she uttered as she realised and grasped his hand.

He smiled a broad wide smile. "You're not going to be this timid around Adam, are you? I mean Barbara assured me you would be able to deal with him."

"I am not timid!" TJ defended herself, standing a little taller. "I am merely ensuring that my cameras get to the location in one piece. I would hate to have to sue Mr Morgan for damages before I have even set foot through the door." She bit her tongue, damn her outburst and only in the first three minutes it had reared its ugly head.

The man, however, nodded his approval. "That's more like it. Please, I assure you I will be very careful with it but if my word is insufficient, then I will show you to your room first and you can stash it all away safely yourself."

TJ now returned his smile; she did not think he was taking it offensively, and picking up the handle of her case once more she followed him to a small door at the side of the main double doors. She offered her key card to him, and he opened the door for her.

"I am Andrew Hasrock, Adam's business manager and consultant on all matters business related." He handed her a business card. "If you need anything or

have any questions please let me know, all my contact details are on that card."
"Thanks."

TJ inspected the room, it was beautiful. Clean white walls were dressed with delicate green fabrics, the largest bed she had ever seen dominated the floor and there was a small bathroom off to the side. "This is his spare room?"
"Yes, it's lovely, isn't it, I have spent many a happy night in here whilst Adam and I have been discussing business until the small hours. Speaking of Adam, I guess we had better get this over and done with."

TJ bit her lip; what was it with this guy? Everyone seemed to be petrified of him, how bad could he be? Sucking up her courage, she took a deep breath and followed Andrew out of the room. "The connecting doors are locked from both sides; we haven't got over that hurdle yet." He whispered to her, chuckling slightly. "Right, here we go."

As the doors opened so did TJ's mouth; only in the movies had she ever seen a place like this. A complete open plan living area met her eyes first, the wall made up completely of glass, the city displayed like a piece of art before her. Large white sofas were surrounded by oversized green plants and small tables. There was a huddle of people over by the table to the right and they all began to part, like a curtain, revealing Adam examining all the paperwork in front of him.

"Adam, this is..." Andrew began.

"I know who it is, thank you, there is no need for introductions. Andrew."

TJ swallowed hard, time to turn on the charm.

"Mr Morgan, I would like to thank you for this opportunity to work with you and..." She paused as his crystal blue eyes turned on her, looking her up and down. "...Erm...well." She tried to refocus as her mind suddenly went blank. "I just wanted to say that I assure you I will be completely professional and will not invade your privacy."

"Your very presence is invading my privacy, Ms Knapley." He snarled and TJ found herself taking a step back.

"Now come on, Adam, we agreed," Andrew butted in.

"We agreed nothing - you agreed - you and my mother hatched this scheme up, SHE is nothing to do with me!"

Andrew was about to complain again when TJ felt a surge of annoyance.

"Now just hold on, mister, I have just met you, whether you hired me or not the polite thing to do is to return a greeting. Pissed or not. Your mother brought you up better than that!" A gasp could be heard from everyone around him, and again she faltered as Adam rose to his feet.

"My mother!" he repeated, "and what exactly would you know about my mother!"

Unperturbed, TJ stood facing him. His large frame towered above her. "I know enough to know I like her and I do not like you!" she spat.

The room was silent watching the two square off to each other, and TJ's heart was beating so hard she swore he could see it pounding through her chest as he stood motionless just staring at her in disbelief.
"I could fire you right now, you know," he counteracted.
"I think we have already established that YOU didn't hire me, your mother did, so you know what, good luck, I'll just wait in my room whilst you phone her and get her to fire me."

Confidence was brewing in her veins as she turned her heel and left the stunned group, heading towards her little room. She winked at Andrew as she passed him, watching him struggling to hide his smile.
"Wait!" Adam called out after her.
TJ stopped and without even turning said, "Giving in already, bloody hell, Adam, I was led to believe you would be a challenge. That was just downright boring. I will go unpack, shall I?" Andrew was now holding his sides as TJ slammed the door behind her and he heard her open her own door, slamming that one for effect.

"It's not funny, Andrew," Adam complained.
"No, not at all is it funny, Adam, you getting your arse whipped by a young girl – no, definitely nothing

funny about that! Excuse me a minute." He walked into the office and Adam heard him let out a large tummy-rumbling laugh, his face screwed up in disgust. "Sorry, just had to get that out," he chuckled as he returned. He had long since learned that Adam's bark had no bite to it.

Adam was not amused, he did not like strangers poking their noses into his business and this one was obviously overly nosy with an attitude to boot.

This was going to be a nightmare.

TJ sat on the edge of the bed shaking when Andrew gingerly knocked and entered.
"Who the hell does that prick think he is?" TJ was livid that he had made her feel like that; she was here to do a job, not get a ton of abuse for doing it.
"TJ, listen to me, that 'prick' is the reason why you are here and the reason you are getting paid and the reason you will get a heap of work afterwards. I saw you, you can handle yourself, you don't need me to hold your hand in there, so get your arse up and start working." Andrew stood up and before leaving gave TJ a peck on the top of her head. The act shocked her and she looked up at him; he was smiling affectionately and she was helpless in the face of his charm.

"This is going to be a nightmare, isn't it?" TJ muttered.

"Nightmare would be an understatement, Suze," TJ said as she recalled the day's events back to her friend. "He was a total pain in the arse. He practically growled at me every time I tried to get anywhere near him - it's useless, I have got nothing at all to work with today."

"Oh come on! TJ, you got to stare at Adam Morgan all day long - life is not that bad!"

"Suze, you have no idea, the man is a total prat. He is so far up his own arse he can no longer see daylight." Suzy spat the wine out that she was drinking, laughing hysterically.

"TJ, you are awful."

The two friends spoke a little longer before Suzy finally had to go as she was heading out for a hot date.

"Who are you going out with?" TJ asked, she had no idea that Suzy had her eye on anyone.

"Erm, you know that guy that scared you the other night when you put the bins out?"

"Suze, you are joking?"

"TJ, it was a misunderstanding, he had a bit too much to drink and he came on a bit strong. He came over to apologise as soon as he sobered up. I'm telling you, he was really upset about the whole thing." TJ groaned in disbelief. "TJ, please, he is really nice."

"Unbelievable, Suze, you be careful, do whatever you want. I have to go, I have work to do."

"TJ, please don't be mad," Suzy pleaded.

"I'm not, enjoy your date."

But that was a big fat lie, she was mad, mad to the point of 'smashing up this pristine pretty apartment' mad. What was Suzy thinking? The guy had grabbed her, acted like a total dick; so of course, her roommate was going on a date with him.

She threw her phone onto her bed in frustration; she had had a crap day and now was having a crap evening. Adam had acted like a spoilt child all day, TJ had tried to get some shots of him working, maybe even a sly smile but no. He had done all he could to block his face from her, positioning people between them. At two pm they had made the journey to his office which was all of a seven-minute drive away, he had introduced her to everyone as 'BJ the student'. When she had tried to correct him he had said,
"I thought you were to be seen and not heard, we are to imagine that you are not really here," and he had done exactly that. Every time he had been offered coffee, she was not, and every time he offered to hold the door, it was slammed in her face.

It got old and boring really quickly.

Now here she was alone in the apartment, all the employees had gone home and Adam was 'out', that was all she knew. At least Andrew had left the adjoining rooms open so that TJ could get some pictures of the apartment without the distinctive chill Adam's presence seemed to bring.

TJ slid open the balcony doors and stepped out onto a large patio area that overlooked the whole city. If it was not for Adam himself, TJ would have loved staying here, the apartment itself was huge and completely open plan. There was a large breakfast bar that separated the living area from the kitchen, which was state of the art.

TJ had opted out of the dinner invitation from Andrew, and instead made herself a triple decker sandwich from the fridge that was stacked to the brim with all sorts of foods TJ didn't even recognise. Having no idea how to work the space age dishwasher, she had hand-washed her plates and left them to drain.

Outside was amazing, there was a small bar and barbeque area (not that she could ever see Adam barbequing), chairs and tables and beautiful delicate plants and flowers. It was a strange contrast to the harsh, almost clinical interior. Placing her can of coke on the outside table, she raised her camera and began to truly see everything, the city a blur of lights beneath her, the soft gentle glow of the moon smudging the night sky. Her camera whirled as she took in every little detail, every scene captured for her to review at any time. She slowly turned, viewing the bar and planted areas through the patio doors that she had slightly shut behind her.

"Shit," she hissed out as through the lens she saw Adam entering the apartment; he was not alone.

"Crap - now what do I do?" TJ whispered to herself, she reached for her mobile, only to realise that it was still on her bed, where she had thrown it after speaking to Suzy. There was nothing else to do, she would have to just apologise and get out of there as soon as possible.

She stood up and picked up her camera, and sucking in a deep breath of courage, she turned to go inside but stopped in her tracks. Adam was no longer making the woman a drink and, TJ was guessing from the way he had his hands all over her, they were more than just friends. Damn, if she walked in now it would seem like she was spying on him and he would have her sacked on the spot, she had promised his mother that she would respect his privacy. Now she was stuck out there until they decided to take it to the bedroom. God knows how long that would be.

It had been a full thirty minutes since TJ had seen Adam and his girlfriend, and she hoped that they might have moved into a bedroom by now as her bottom was now numb from sitting on the cold, hard floor. Unable to see, she picked up her camera and viewed through the lens hoping to see into the dark room better. They had not moved it into the bedroom; instead Adam had the woman pressed firmly against the living room wall, his kisses frantic and desperate. TJ would never have imagined him being so passionate, she thought he would be a 'strictly in the bed' sort of guy, but here he was acting so desperate, so needy. She knew she shouldn't watch, but somehow she seemed unable to tear herself away.

With one hand, Adam grasped the woman's hands and held them above her head, his free hand slowly rising up her thigh. TJ shifted uncomfortably, a need suddenly arising from deep within, causing hot flushes to burn her face. Adam no longer seemed the stiff, proper businessman TJ had met earlier; she watched his head falling back slightly as the woman wrapped her leg around him, pulling him into her. He wasted no time, and freeing her hands trailed his other hand to the back of her knees, pulling slightly so that the second leg took up its position around his waist, suspending the woman off the floor. Her whole weight rested effortlessly on Adam, who was now kissing down the woman's neck and throat, his hands firmly holding her buttocks tightly. Without realising it, TJ's breathing had become heavy and her mouth dry as she watched the pair entwined in a passionate embrace. Unconsciously she pressed the button on her camera, a series of moments were captured. "Shit," she cursed but still she did not turn away. Adam's hands were now exploring lower, he was not gentle or slow and the woman's head was thrown back in sheer delight; at this point TJ spun around wondering what the hell she was doing.

Flinging her back against the wall, she slid down into a sitting position, her head in her hands in disgust. What was she doing? Why didn't she just go inside when she first saw them come in? To make it worse she had taken pictures, she had stood there spying and taking pictures of the man! If it had been the other way around she would have been furious, disgusted even.

She stared out at the patio, listening to the traffic, trying to distract herself from what she could only imagine was happening inside.

And oh boy, could she imagine.

Chapter 6

ADAM REACHED OUT HIS hand to her. "You're freezing," he crooned.

"I fell asleep," TJ admitted. Adam tilted his head and smiled playfully but before TJ could protest he pulled her into a tight embrace, his strong arms pushing her back to the wall. "Adam, I don't think..." He silenced her with a gentle kiss. She unwillingly groaned into his mouth and that was all the encouragement he needed. Grasping her waist, he pinned her against the wall kissing her neck and throat, and began moving down.

"Oh, Adam," TJ sighed.

"TJ," he called out. "TJ...TJ, wake up!"

TJ slowly opened her eyes to see Adam crouched down next to her. "Is your room not to your high and mighty standards?" TJ frantically scanned around her, confused and disorientated. Oh God, she was still on the balcony, she must have fallen asleep out here, what must he think of her?

"I'm sorry, I was taking pictures of the view and I must have fallen asleep out here."

"Mmm, and were dreaming, I presume." A smug smile uglied his face and TJ's glowed red in embarrassment. "You were erm...muttering things in your sleep." If possible his smug grin grew and TJ closed her eyes, hoping the world would just swallow her up now.

"I was taking pictures out here, I guess I lost track of time." She desperately tried to change the subject, snatching the coffee cup that he held out to her.

"Pictures, eh!" he muttered.

"Yes. That is what I am here to do, Mr Morgan, take pictures. Not that you would know after yesterday."

Adam scowled and turned back into the apartment, leaving TJ to try and stretch out all of her muscles, which were all now scrunched up and sore as hell. Taking a sip of the delicious liquid gold, she stooped down to pick up her camera.

"Oh shit! Bastard!" Her camera was missing.

Adam's eyes lifted to meet her as she ran into the apartment and registered her camera sitting on the table, hooked up to his laptop.

"I can explain!" she began.

"Really? You can explain ...this one." He slowly turned the laptop around and TJ came face to face with a full screen picture of Adam's mouth firmly attached to the woman's neck. Not only had she taken the photos, she had actually zoomed in, focused on every tiny little detail of his face, every expression. TJ had never felt so ashamed in her life;

she had no idea what had possessed her last night. He was going to ensure she was fired now, ensure that everyone knew she was trash, and she would never get work again. Her heart sank and tears pooled in her eyes.

"No, I can't explain my actions, Mr Morgan. I shall pack my things up and leave, I will understand if you want to press charges."

She waited for the fiery dragon to appear, for the temper that everyone talked about to rise and attack but instead he just returned to the screen.

"There's none of her face, I don't think she would be happy about that," he uttered, distracted. "There are, however ... a lot ... of my face." His eyes returned to hers as he spoke and he rested his chin onto his hand, awaiting her response. He should have been furious, livid that she had dared to take these images, but instead he found himself a little turned on, especially after listening to her moaning his name in her sleep.

"I didn't find her an interesting subject," TJ managed.

"Is this what you were dreaming about TJ? Me, doing this, to you?"

TJ's mouth fell open, "No of course not! I mean...how dare you presume that just because I took pictures of you I fancy you! Jesus, you really are an ego on legs, aren't you!"

Her voice began to get louder and louder. "Christ, I spent all day following you around, you are like a robot, emotionless, cool and efficient. I took those because your face was the most animated it had been all day, and you almost looked human for a change!" She caught her breath, panting as she ended her rant, her voice echoing round the room.

"Come here!" Adam ordered.

"No. I am not your pet."

"TJ, come here...please."

TJ was knocked off balance; she did not understand this change of tactics.

"TJ, these pictures, they really are quite beautiful. You have captured some very heated emotions."

"Yeah well. It wasn't hard to do," she said sarcastically.

"Really?" he questioned. "Because I really didn't feel anything like this with her, and I severely doubt that she was doing anything else but going through the motions."

Her face contorted with confusion.

"So, how is it, Ms. Knapley, that you have managed to portray such eroticism in these images. Could it be that you were aroused yourself?"

"Don't be disgusting!" she shouted back, enraged that he would think that.

"Really? *Oh Adam,*" he mimicked, "*Oh Adam yes...there!*"

"Oh piss off!" TJ screeched, and ran to her bedroom as quickly as possible.

TJ felt no better despite the long hot shower she had endured, scrubbing her skin pink. She sat on the edge of the large bed that she had not even slept in yet; cold wet droplets of water fell from her hair, causing her to shiver as they trickled down her back.

"What an arsehole!" she cursed aloud, not really sure if she was talking about him or herself.

How did she get herself into these predicaments? Other people seemed to manage to go through life quite easily without messing up every two minutes but, TJ. Oh no, TJ had to cause the most stupid, unnecessary problems possible with her ridiculous behaviour.

"TJ?" A gentle knock at the connecting door caused her to shake herself out of her self-pity.

"What?" she snapped.

"Open the door ... please, I have brought you some breakfast."

TJ's stomach grumbled its approval of this idea and so she slid off the bed and opened the door.

"It wasn't locked."

"I know, but I didn't want to be presumptuous or rude....my mother brought me up better than that."

TJ fought a smile as he repeated her words back to her.

"Come on, please, can we start again. I was a prat, you were a nosy bitch, so let's drop all the defences and start again."

After a plate of toast, fruit and, of course, a few cups of coffee, TJ was feeling a lot better. Adam had almost become human and they were chatting about his business, like old friends. TJ once more apologised for the photos and assured him she was not spying on him. She had just been in the wrong place at the wrong time. He accepted her apology and they agreed to start again.

"Do you fancy going somewhere today? I mean it's Sunday so no one is working."

"Erm sure, I mean I am being paid to take photos of you, so yeah, sure."

Adam began clearing up the plates. "No cameras, just me and you out for the day. A 'get to know each other' sort of thing. Only you need to wear more than just that towel." He chuckled as he stood to leave.

"I have been sitting in this towel all through breakfast and it hasn't bothered you." A cheeky smile slipped from her lips.

"Oh it's bothered me, Tabby Cat, BELIEVE ME, it has bothered me. I am just too much of a gentleman to say it."

TJ's face once again began to resemble the colour of a good claret, but this time it was a pleasant sensation.

She quickly dressed in her traditional uniform of jeans and vest then headed into the lounge where Adam was sitting at the table waiting for her. She slid into the seat opposite,

"So what's with the 'Tabby Cat' name?"

Adam knotted his hands together and placed both elbows on the table, resting his chin once more, leaning in staring straight into her eyes.

"If you choose to sleep outside like a stray cat - what else am I to call you?" He stared continuously, trying to gauge her reaction.

"You're never going to let me forget this, are you?"

Adam shook his head, his eyes glinting mischievously.

"And so, every time you call me that..."

"You are going to be reminded of the effect I had on you," he finished for her.

"God, you really are a walking dick, aren't you. Maybe it was just a dream; maybe you were just rubbing my feet or something." Adam let out a little chuckle.

"Note to self - she likes foot rubs."

"No I didn't mean...I was just saying...Oh, bog off!"

He held out a hand. "Come on, enough playing, let's get out of here."

Wherever TJ had imagined that they were going to go - it certainly wasn't here. Adam pulled the car into a huge driveway and after a short drive they had pulled up outside a dog rescue centre. He stilled the engine and turned to her.

"Okay, I give in - are you getting a dog?"

"No, this is a little hobby of mine. Very few people know about this, TJ, so I am asking you to be respectful of that." His eyes widened and TJ suddenly felt intrusive, which was weird considering what she had witnessed the night before.

"I promise," she agreed.

A sigh of relief escaped his lips and he jumped out of the car to open the door for her.

The place was not large by any means, not one of the big; well-known centres, it had a farm sort of feel to it. Surrounded by fields and tall trees, the building was nestled back against a hillside, it felt like a million miles away from the city, that was just down the road. She could see instantly why Adam liked it here.

"Adam! I didn't know you were coming here today," a woman called out, striding over from the reception area. Adam greeted the woman with a warm hug and turned to introduce TJ.
"This is TJ; she is shadowing me for a while - a work thing. TJ, this is Malika, she runs the centre here."

Malika was a tiny little woman, barely reaching Adam's chest but the glare she gave TJ was poisonous. "And you brought her here?" she asked in disbelief.
"She's taking some pictures of me, that's all, she's not a suit," he whispered low and sultry. Malika visibly relaxed a little and uttered a gruff, standoffish 'hello'.

The reception area was more like a staff room than the smart, clean reception TJ had expected, staff were scattered all over the room on mismatched chairs and desks. They all looked up as she entered but then seeing Adam follow her in, all eyes turned to him and a cheer of greetings rang out.

It was hypnotic watching the change in this man, he had been so stiff and formal yesterday but today, here, he was a completely different person. He greeted each person warmly and shook hands, chatting to each one in turn. Finally he turned to introduce TJ and again she received a frosty reception. What was it with this guy? She felt like they were all protecting him like a pack of animals.

"What is a successful man like you doing hanging out in a place like this?" she asked. Adam seemed to glow as he greeted them affectionately but before he could speak Malika stepped in.

"First of all - a place like what? You don't like my place?"

"Keep your fake wig on," TJ replied. "I mean, the side of Adam I have seen is a suit, a man who keeps his distance from everyone, cool, calculated. Here, it's like coming home for a family dinner, complete with kids running around making a mess and no one caring."

Malika stood aghast. "I have never heard a better description of my place in all my years of being here." She turned to Adam, "I like her, Adam...I like her a lot. She has fire and gumption."

"You have no idea," Adam muttered.

After kitting her out in a full paper suit, Malika agreed to give TJ the full tour of her place. She told her that they were completely reliant on donations to run her centre, patrons like Adam donated funds to pay for the building, staff and of course all the food and vets' bills. They took in abandoned animals or injured animals - mostly dogs, on a few occasions they had been handed dogs by people who could no longer care for them but, unfortunately, most of the dogs in the centre had been victims of abuse.

They arrived at one of the kennels and Malika opened the door; as TJ peered in, her eyes immediately filled with painful tears.

"This here is Bristles." A tiny little brown dog looked up from its bed, his ribs clearly visible and his tail nothing but a string, but still his huge brown eyes widened and his tail thumped the floor loudly. TJ bent down to greet the little pup.

"He was found on a rubbish tip, he was so thin his eyes were sunk right back into his head, we had to completely shave him due to the fleas, but we are looking after him now. He has put on weight and we named him Bristles, because he is all spiky like a brush where his hair is growing back," Malika explained.

The pup began licking TJ's face, clearing away the tears that were pouring from her eyes.

"He is so beautiful," she muttered, turning her head to avoid the pup smothering her.

The next kennel provided no relief for TJ, as a greyhound stood leaning against the wall, its back to her but again the ribs were sticking out through its skin. There were obvious burns along its back and one of its legs was very crooked.

"This is Ghost. He was brought back from the edge, I don't know how the vet did it, because I was sure he wouldn't make it... but he did."

"What happened to him?" TJ asked gingerly, not really sure she wanted to know.

"This guy was neglected, starved, probably turned out onto the streets after a life in racing. Then some kids found him and decided it would be fun to pour petrol all over his back and set it alight."

TJ clasped her hand over her mouth as she let out a cry. The dog slowly turned, hearing the noise. His tail was not wagging like the dog before had, instead it hung low and the haunted eyes of the poor skeleton-like dog burned into her soul.

"I am so sorry, Ghost," TJ cried. "I do not know why someone would do this to you, but you are okay now. You are safe." She reached out her hand, low and practically on the ground; she did not rush for fear of scaring the animal and turned her eyes away to the side. Slowly, very slowly, Ghost moved a little closer and gently placed his muzzle into her hand, sniffing as he did. She fought the urge to reach out and cuddle the poor creature; she wanted so desperately to give the love he deserved to have. After what seemed like an eternity, the dog moved to stand next to her and without warning he replaced the wall with her. TJ nearly lost her balance and shot one hand out to the side to steady herself as the dog leant his full weight against her, never looking at her; he just continued to stare straight ahead as TJ silently sobbed next to him. Malika turned to Adam and closed the kennel door.

"Right, hotshot - who the hell is she?" Malika demanded to know once they had reached the privacy of her little office.
"What? I told you she's here to take some photos of me, my mother's idea. I just thought she might like to see it here."
Malika eyed him suspiciously.
"That dog has not so much as given any of the staff a second glance since he has been here, let alone allowed anyone to touch him. She is here one minute and walks in and bonds with him immediately... I mean - Christ, Adam!"

Adam had to admit the way she had reacted with the dogs had hit his heart hard. He had kind of expected her to be a bit squeamish and hesitant, but TJ had just got straight in there. Sat on the dirty floor and allowed the dogs to lick all her makeup off, she was not like any other girl he had dated before.

Not that he was dating TJ!

Dogs had a good instinct about people; he had learnt that early on; if the dogs trusted TJ then maybe he should give her a break and trust her too.

Opening the kennel door, he was amazed to see TJ still in the same position, Ghost leaning fully against her.

"Your legs must be killing you by now," he joked but as TJ raised her face up towards him, his heart fell apart. She was still crying, tears pouring from her eyes from the simple connection that she had made. "Come on," he gently offered. "He will be cared for here."

TJ slowly began to stand, trying to move Ghost off her; he staggered a little then resumed his position against the wall. He stood motionless once more just staring out, his comfortable fluffy bed left unslept in.

"How can anyone do that?" TJ wailed as Adam held her against his chest once they were clear of the kennel. "How could they hurt that beautiful animal? He is so gentle."

Adam could not answer her; he was unable to answer her. From being young he had loved all animals, had numerous pets and could not imagine what would possess someone to want to hurt these creatures.
"Come on; let's see some of the other ones here."
"I don't think my heart can take anymore." TJ attempted to stem the flow as she gathered herself together.
"Trust me." Holding his hand against her face as he spoke, he kissed her sweetly on her tear-soaked cheek.

Chapter 7

Adam laughed as TJ struggled to hold the two little puppies that were wriggling around in her arms. "Ying and Yang came to us from a lady who just couldn't afford them; they already have homes. Malika just needs to go check the new owners out."

"She goes to check them out?" TJ could only guess the strict rules she had for new owners.

"She visits the home, makes sure it's appropriate because loving a dog is just a small part. She likes to make sure that all her babies go to good homes, but more importantly the right homes for them."

TJ understood, she felt protective just holding these little angels in her arms. Adam reached over and scratched the ear of the little black pup, who immediately began to whimper, trying to get across to him.

"I see Barnaby is asleep, again," he said, talking to the dog as he took her from TJ. She examined the floor, not having noticed another pup in this kennel; her eyes suddenly spotted the food bowl and sure enough, curled up right inside it was a fat, little gold puppy.

"Oh my God, that is just too cute." She leaned over and gently lifted Barnaby out of the food bowl; the other puppies now on the floor raced over and began to gobble down the food quickly. Adam let out a loud laugh that sent TJ into chuckles of delight with him.

"Do you know he was found by a farmer, suckling on one of the sheep? Can you believe it? Greedy little thing he is. Look at the size of him." His words were harsh but the kisses he was raining down on the fat, little ones belly, relayed his true feelings.

"I could stay here all day," TJ admitted as she shed her paper suit.

She had really shocked Adam, not just by the way she had been around the dogs, or the way they had reacted to her, but also that she just got straight to it. Cleaning out kennels, picking up all their mess, running around playing with them, it had been a real eye opener for him.

"Yeah - I love it here. I can relax and I get a real sense of achievement here, like I am making a difference."

"You don't get that from the cafés?"

In a gentle but dismissive way he replied, "it's different." That was the only explanation he was prepared to give her.

"You hungry?"

"I am starving"

"I know a really good bar just round the corner - does a mean steak."

TJ closed her eyes, her mouth watering just thinking about delicious steak. Without her realising it the day had just flown by and without lunch inside her, TJ's stomach was NOT happy.

Adam was mesmerised watching TJ slowly lick her lips. Her eyes fluttered and closed and her now moist lips glistened in the sunlight. This woman was beginning to get under his skin, everything about her intrigued him, he was hooked the minute she had fought back at him at their first meeting but after today... he was starting to have feelings, feelings he had never felt with a woman before. But then again, he had never met a woman like TJ before.

"Oh no, you are not leaving without seeing that dog!" Malika came out to the car where they were both standing. "You know damn well that dog has caught your scent and is now tearing up the place, so you can just delay your little mating ritual and get your arse in to see that dog!"

Adam explained that a few months ago a large dog had been brought into the centre, he was uncontrollable and no one had been able to handle him, so the poor pup had been homed and re-homed and every time they just brought him straight back. Because of this, for one reason or another, 'Bulldog' had decided that Adam, was his owner and so pined in his absence and delighted in his return; he was the only one that Bulldog remotely behaved for.

"I'd better go see him before I leave; will you be alright for ten minutes?"
"Sure." TJ watched him go back into the centre and heaved a sigh of relief, she knew she was attracted to him, who wouldn't be, he was a gorgeous specimen but now, now he had this soft side. Groaning, she leant back onto the bonnet of his car.

"Oh my, I know that look." Malika had been watching her. "You've gone and fallen for my man, haven't you."
"Don't be ridiculous, I have only just met him."
Malika just huffed. "That boy is like family to me and I am fiercely protective of my family."

TJ admired and respected him even more, knowing that Adam surrounded himself with all these strong, protective women; it only gave him more brownie points in her eyes. Malika invited her in for tea whilst she waited and seated her in her little office, from in there she could hear loud barking and Adam's laughter echoing from down the halls.

"He has been a benefactor of ours for a while now," Malika told her whilst handing her a chipped mug of tea.
"He came here when he was a young boy, I paid him when I could, but mostly he did volunteer shifts here. After his business became successful he

started donating money every month, regular as clockwork." She examined TJ's face, every reaction and expression processed and translated.

What could TJ say? He seemed to be a wonderful man, warm-hearted, generous, a real 'too good to be true' sort of man.

"So you two are...what?"

"Nothing," TJ answered a little too quickly.

"You don't like my man?"

"Yes...I mean no... I mean, I am working with him at the moment." None of it was believable, she fancied the pants off the man, she had already had a delicious dream about him and was now sharing a day in his company; even more, she was loving every minute of it.

Lost in her own thoughts she screamed as something tickled her elbow, and turned to see the tiniest kitten she had ever seen in her life meowing at her.

"That's Aslan. Just wandered right in through the front door last week, now he runs the place. With me, of course." Malika roared with laughter at her own joke and the little kitten stood up onto its tiptoes, its tail bolt upright. "You wanna see something really funny?" she asked TJ, who nodded playfully.

Adam was filthy, Bulldog had jumped all over him leaving black footprints everywhere, he also had a huge bruise coming up on his elbow, where the beast had thrown him into the wall. But now he had calmed a little, his initial excitement at seeing Adam subdued and now the weight of the dog was rested on Adam's legs as he sat squarely in the middle of his lap.

"Bulldog, you know you are not a lap dog, mate," Adam complained but Bulldog just turned, gave him a wet lick and returned to face outwards perusing his garden. Girlish giggling made him jump and sent Bulldog off again, barking and jumping up wildly.

"Bloody hell; is it a dog or a horse?" TJ yelled out, drowned out by the loud barking and a little intimidated by the huge beast launching itself at the door making it rattle and shake violently.

"Watch this," Malika said, and she reached into her pocket, pulling out the little kitten.

"Oh my God, no don't," TJ called out; already the beast was backing away from the door. TJ watched in amazement as the little kitten strutted into the kennel, its tail bushed up, pointing to the ceiling. But the amazing part was Bulldog's behaviour; the huge dog stopped barking, calmed right down and began following the little kitten around like a shadow. Even when the cocky little cat went over to his food bowl and began helping himself to the food, the monster just sat down and watched it.

"You're pathetic, Bulldog!" Adam declared.

"Why is he called Bulldog?" TJ asked as she watched the kitten make itself at home in the dog's bed. He definitely was not a bulldog breed, his head alone was the size of a beach ball and standing on all fours he was already up to TJ's waist, so on two paws he would tower over her.

"His nickname stuck, he was classed as 'a bull in a china shop', everyone just kept sending him back, he is clumsy and causes damage and is just so big." Malika sighed sadly. She knew he would not find another home now; there had been too many owners and too many returns.

"They just don't understand you, do they, boy?" Adam fussed as he stood to leave. "After all you're still a puppy, aren't you?"

"A puppy!" TJ called out. "You are joking! He is gonna get bigger!"

Adam and Malika just laughed but as Adam retrieved Aslan and closed the door, TJ felt the atmosphere become heavy and heard the pine from Bulldog as they walked away.

"It must be hard, leaving him there." TJ took another sip of her wine and cut off another piece of the delicious steak. Adam had been very quiet all the way to the restaurant and she guessed he was sad at leaving Bulldog upset. Adam nodded. "Can't you adopt him?" she asked innocently.

Adam snorted. "Yes, I can really see that dog fitting into my life! I'm sorry, I don't mean to snap, I just wish I could find him a good home, that's all."

TJ reached across and held his hand, her fingers stroking along the skin. He watched her cautiously, not really knowing how to respond.

"Thank you for today," she said, removing her hand, much to his dismay.

"You are welcome. I am glad you enjoyed it."

Something was happening, they both knew it. It felt as if the air all around them was crackling, sparks flying in all directions, the air so heavy making it hard to breathe.

"So, what is on the menu for tomorrow?" TJ tried to distract herself. "Are you going to let me take some pictures?"

He sat back in his chair defensively. His arms folded themselves across his chest. After a long, deathly silence he finally announced, "You do seem to bring out the best in me. I guess it would be nice to have you around a bit longer."

TJ's heart flipped at the signals he was giving, it took every ounce of restraint she had not to leap over the table and kiss him right there and then. But she was working.

"Just till Tuesday," she blurted out. "I mean I am working for you at the minute, aren't I. You hired me till Tuesday to get some decent shots, so that is all I can do, I mean should do." Rapidly she returned to cutting her meat and stuffing it in her mouth, suddenly needing something to do. Adam, however, felt no need; he remained leaning back, watching her with interest.

"I thought we had already established that 'I' didn't hire you, therefore if 'I' can't fire you then you certainly don't work FOR me in any way shape or form. But I understand your need to keep things on a professional basis, I get where you are coming from." With his speech concluded he returned to his meal.

Shit, TJ thought, *what did I just agree to?*

"So my mother is having a charity do on Friday and I wondered as you will no longer be working for my mother, if you might like to attend with me?" Again TJ's stomach turned over.

"Like on a date sort of thing?"

"Like a charity invitation sort of thing, TJ, I know you are obsessed with me but I have not yet made up my mind about you!"

"What!" TJ cried out, causing every diner to turn and stare at the rude interruption to their meal. "How dare ..."

Her stream of insults was cut short as she saw the playful grin he now displayed whilst enjoying his steak.

"Shit, I walked straight into that one," she complained, more to herself than Adam. "I will think about it and let you know." *Ha, strike to me*, she thought but Adam just winked and summoned the waitress to bring over another bottle of wine.

Chapter 8

THE NEXT FEW DAYS whirled past in a blur; Adam's life was certainly hectic. Meetings, promotions, stock reviews, the list was endless. By the time he had finished on Monday it was late and all she was capable of doing was climbing into her bed and immediately falling asleep. But now, she was nearing the end of her last day and although she had got some great shots of Adam at work and no doubt his business partners would be over the moon with them, she had no shots that his mother had asked for.

Driving back from the office, Adam was distracted as usual by his phone and its endless text lists and emails. He sensed her watching him.

"You okay?" he asked.

TJ just nodded.

"Bored?"

She smiled.

"What say we just call it me and you tonight, a takeaway and a film?"

"As much as I would love that, I don't have all the pictures of you that I need. I had something else in mind."

A look of worry and intrigue spread across his face, if TJ was planning it - it could not be good.

"Really?" he questioned as TJ opened the door to The Coffee Café and immediately slipped into a booth. "Like I don't see enough of this place during the day?"

"Yes, but I want to know about it, why you started it etc?"

"Mmm, pictures AND an interview?"

"Oh my God, it's you, I knew it, it's you!" a voice shrieked out, and TJ cringed.

"Sorry," she said before Suzy had even reached the table.

Adam just smiled that dazzling smile. "Someone you know?"

"My flatmate." TJ rolled her eyes, dreading the embarrassment Suzy was bound to cause her.

Suzy bounded over, grinning ear to ear. "I should be cross because you haven't texted me, but bringing this delicious morsel to me is more than enough!" Squeezing herself into the booth next to TJ, Suzy plonked her drink onto the table. "So what are we up to tonight?"

"I was just about to retell the story of my life," Adam revealed, flashing that winning grin at Suzy who was now fluttering her eyelashes wildly. "But first, let's order some more drinks."

Adam explained that he had lost his brother when he was just eight years old, he did not go into details but TJ got the impression it was alcohol-related. It had a huge impact on him and as a result he decided he wanted to open a place where people could hang out. Not a pub that was purely alcohol-based, somewhere people could meet and choose to either drink or not drink.

"I met up with Andrew after a friend of my father's had recommended him and he took care of the business and figures side, as I have no head for all that. I left school at sixteen and worked every job possible to get the money together and several years later - here we are." He paused to take a sip of his coffee.

"But you do have a licence? I mean there is alcohol served in the back, isn't there?" Suzy asked.

This was news to TJ, she didn't even know that there was a back room and immediately wanted to go see. Adam collected their cups and offered the tour. As soon as they entered, staff suddenly began to fluster about cleaning things! TJ was stunned that she had never been in here. A long wooden bar stretched the length of the room and stools lined up along it, there were two pool tables against the back wall and a number of tables and chairs. It was like a pub and a man cave all rolled into one.

"Have you never been in this part, TJ?" Adam asked.

"Never thought to come here at night," she admitted. "It's just amazing."

He smiled, suddenly feeling very proud of his first café.

"You can have beer or spirits here, but you can also order coffee, tea or anything you want." He observed TJ carefully. "Go on then."

"Eh?" Her face contorted in confusion.

"You, camera, pictures. I can almost see your fingers twitching for it."

Suzy giggled and headed for the bar, ordering three beers.

TJ took out her camera and began snapping away at everything her eyes came across; she loved it, not just what she saw, but the atmosphere also, it was electric. Everyone laughing and talking, choosing songs on the jukebox or playing arcade games. Guitars hung from the walls next to portraits of their previous owners, there were framed letters from grateful customers and over the bar was suspended a huge surfboard.

Suzy immediately headed for the pool table that was now vacant and persuaded Adam to join her; the lens was drawn to Adam as he shrugged off his jacket and slowly slid the knot of his tie down. Frame after frame TJ studied this man, watched him slowly uncoil, removing the business persona that he displayed daily and replacing it with a fun, relaxed, playful man. Suddenly Adam threw his head back in laughter, Suzy had said something that had reduced them to hysterics, and again TJ frantically took her photos, unable to get enough as she drank in the magnificence of this sexy man. Her heart thumped as she captured every movement, every expression; he was the most exquisite creature she had ever known.

Adam had felt at ease at first, he was enjoying Suzy's company but knowing that TJ was watching, capturing everything he did was beginning to unnerve the hell out of him. That was until Suzy walked across to him and put his mind at rest.

"She fancies the arse off you, you know."

Adam let out a snigger. "Yes I think so too. However, she has yet to admit it to herself."

"Judging by the amount of time she has spent fawning over you, I am sure she is fighting as much as possible but believe me, the way she is looking at you right now, it's not hard to see." Suzy nodded her head over to TJ who was still wholly focused on Adam.

"It's embarrassing," he admitted slowly.

"From what I have heard, she has embarrassed herself enough in front of you; it's only fair you return the favour."

Adam was taken back a little. "She told you about that?"

"Told me? By the time she had finished, I nearly got off myself!"

Adam threw his head back in a raucous laugh and Suzy joined him, both laughing till their sides ached, while TJ stood in the background capturing every moment.

After a few hours, Suzy decided to meet up with some of her friends and move somewhere else, leaving Adam and TJ alone.

"Fancy heading out for a meal?" he asked.

"Fancy heading home for a pizza?" she counter-offered.

Adam raised his eyebrow, never before had he offered to take a girl out for a meal only to have her prefer a takeaway and home. Women wanted expensive things, didn't they? Expensive meals and gifts. But TJ, apparently, was quite happy spending the night in.

"You order, I need to get comfy," TJ announced as they exited the lift.

"I don't know what you like." He panicked as she rushed to her own door, leaving him standing outside.

"Anything," she shouted back.

Great! What was he supposed to order, plain and safe? What if she didn't like spicy food? What if she didn't like mushrooms? His head began to pound at the huge responsibility he suddenly felt to order the right topping.

"What is wrong with me?" he muttered as he picked up the phone, "It is just pizza, for goodness sake."

TJ emerged minutes later in white pyjamas covered in bright red poppies. "That's better, I do love my jeans, but I adore my comfies."

Adam swallowed hard as she slumped into the sofa opposite him and curled her legs to the side. The pyjamas were beautiful, a delicate mix of bright colours and large flowers, the tight vest top left little to the imagination and Adam found himself attempting to focus on everything around him to avoid looking at her. Thank God the pizza arrived at that point, but before he could stand TJ had leapt up, grabbing her purse, and answered the door. His blood began to boil as he watched the spotty young man staring at TJ's ample chest, TJ completely unaware as she delved around for some money. The young man took a fleeting glance at Adam, whose face must have displayed the jealous anger he was feeling, because the boy turned scarlet and hot-footed it out of there before TJ could offer a tip.

"What's wrong with you?" TJ asked as she turned to see Adam's expression.
"Nothing," he snapped, confused by his own feelings.
"Blimey, moody or what!" She returned to the sofa.
"How much did it come to?" Adam asked, reaching for his wallet.
"My treat!"
"You are kidding me, right? No way, I will pay."
TJ sat back. "I beg your pardon? Do we not accept gifts from mere women?" Her voice was rising and becoming louder and Adam retracted quickly, recognising the warning signs.
"No, no I just, I mean you're my guest. But hey, if you want to pay that's fine by me. Most women are quite

happy for me to pay for everything but whatever, Tabby Cat!"

"I am not like most women," TJ retorted.

She was not wrong there, Adam had never met anyone like her, it was like she was his equal, she did not see a rich businessman, or an uneducated wannabe, for that matter. She just saw a friend. She tucked into the pizza heartily.

"Mmm perfect, I am starving," she said, her mouth full. "So, talk more."

"About what?" he chuckled. "Me? Surely not more?"

"Not the blurb on the back of your leaflets, about you."

This was it, make or break time; did he brush her off with a few facts or did he open up to her, something he had not done with anyone for a long, long time? He sucked in his breath.

"My brother died when I was eight, he was seventeen- not even old enough to drink - but he got himself involved in a bar brawl. Some idiot took a bottle to his head and that was that. Brian fell, smashed his head and died there and then."

TJ took a sip of the beer he had just handed to her.

"My mum and dad took it hard, they struggled to come to terms with it all but somehow they managed it and came out the other side stronger than ever."

"And what about you?" TJ asked gently, "Did you come out the other side unscathed?"

"Take a look around you. What do you think?"

"I think money isn't everything."

"Ha." Adam spat his beer out. "You would be the first woman I have met to think that!"

"I don't think your mother feels that way either."

"True, no my mother enjoys the money but has never needed it," he replied fondly.

His mother had supported him in all his efforts to succeed, not just to succeed but to ensure that no other young kids suffered the same fate as his brother. But all the way she had insisted that he pursue his own life, found some way to have hobbies and date, not that he had found any of the girls he had dated half as interesting as TJ.

Starting the business had been difficult for him, investors were wary of Adam's lack of education and were unwilling to help, so when he did get offered assistance it usually came at a price. A stream of stuck-up educated toffs that thought they were all so much better than him, so Adam had grown a tough shell to protect himself, surrounded himself with trustworthy friends and rarely let anyone else in. Yet, here he was, talking about his intimate feelings to a woman he had just met.

"So," Adam began turning the spotlight round on her. "Talk!"

TJ put down the piece of pizza she was eating. "Okay, parents are completely loopy, never had an ounce of discipline in my whole life. As a result, was a wild child at school, got into no end of trouble. Suddenly found a love of art and was lucky enough to have a wonderful teacher who invested time in me and showed me I could be worth more than others thought of me. Went to uni, got spotted for an exhibition where I met a wonderful woman who asked me to take pictures of her son!" She leaned in and grabbed the piece of her pizza once more.

"Open book, eh?"

"Yep," she grinned.

"So, the bands on your wrist?"

"Probably the same as you, I have a temper, you have seen it, but I have to say I cannot imagine you losing it like I do."

Adam unconsciously rubbed the wrist where his bands used to be, his mother must have mentioned it. Damn his mother - what else had she revealed about him?

"Anyway, the answer is yes by the way."

Adam was confused, trying to recall what question he had asked her.

"The charity do on Friday, I will go with you. I do not need picking up, I have my own car, so will meet you there if you give me the address."

Nonchalantly she finished off the last piece of pizza and downed her beer. "I need to start packing if I am gonna head off in the morning," she announced, and walked over to the interconnecting door.

"Erm, it will be locked your side," Adam advised her. "You will have to go round."

"Adam, my stubborn businessman, it has NEVER been locked on my side!" She grinned naughtily and swished her hips as she disappeared inside. Adam sat back, his trousers suddenly uncomfortable. God, what was this girl doing to him, he was a complete wreck but damn it if it didn't feel good.

Chapter 9

"OUCH. BLOODY HELL, SUZE, watch the pins!" TJ cried out as another pin nicked the underside of her arm. Suzy muttered something incoherent and continued her design. TJ had been home all of five minutes before she was rummaging through Suzy's collection, needing something to wear for the charity function.

"You are the one that is asking me to alter this with just two days' notice so don't blame me if I pin you in my haste to get it done!"

Suzy and TJ had spent most of her first night home trying to decide what she should wear. Thanks to Suzy's course, TJ had a whole range of outfits, the problem was choosing one. The dresses were beautiful but TJ felt uncomfortable and awkward, plus they made her appear to be making a huge effort for Adam and so they were all out of the window. Suzy had been mortified when TJ had finally announced that she was going to wear jeans.

"Jeans? You are joking! It's a function, for heaven's sake."

"I know that. That also means that most women there will be wearing beautiful, designer dresses costing an arm and a leg, and I don't want to blend in." She paused to make sure Suzy understood. "I want to stand out for all the right reasons."

"And you think jeans are the way to go?"

Suzy had calmed a little when she realised TJ meant the skinny, tight-fitting black jeans she had tucked away in the back of her wardrobe. She had then squealed with delight as she declared she had the exact top to match them. Unfortunately it needed a bit of altering which was the reason TJ felt like a pin cushion with little red dots all the way up her arm.

Suzy cried out triumphantly, "This will be my finest masterpiece, and before you moan I will be taking pictures for my portfolio!" TJ groaned but did not protest; she could not thank Suzy enough for helping her out and she had to admit, in this outfit, she would definitely stand out.

"So, are you going to tell me?" Suzy asked as she finished packing away all her sewing kit and TJ threw her t-shirt back on.

"Tell you what?"

Suzy just stared at her. "Are you in love?" she teased.

"Don't be daft, he's just... you know... he's hot and that!"

"No arguments so far." Suzy handed her a rather large glass of wine. "And...?"

That was an excellent question. She had faltered when she first saw him; his photos really did not do him justice. He was staggeringly handsome, tall, well built, obviously worked out, but more than that, he had an aura about him. She had always ignored her parents when they talked about auras, but Adam had an air of confidence about him that was very attractive, whilst at the same time he was humble and respectful of the people in his life. Suzy still waited for her response.
"I do like him...a lot. I ...think of him ... a lot." An unfamiliar feeling began to flutter in her stomach, not nerves or hunger but whatever it was, it was causing an uncontrollable smile to spread across her face.

Suzy watched in awe, she had never seen TJ like this with anyone and there had been quite a few men since they had moved in together. But now, TJ was grinning and almost glowing as she talked about him. She had confessed to Suzy about the night on the balcony and Suzy had had her suspicions then, but now...now she could see it for herself. TJ was really into this guy.

Friday came around too quickly for TJ's liking, it hadn't helped that she had spent her time perusing all the photos she had taken over the few days. Seeing his face all day every day, having to choose the best of each selection, examining his face making sure she had captured his essence. She was pretty sure they would be happy with the business shots; she had been particularly pleased with the relaxed, cheerful atmosphere that she had managed to create. It portrayed a different side to the strict, all business side everyone knew. But she wanted more than anything to be able to give his mum some pictures of her son.

The night at The Coffee Café had proven to be her saviour; whilst she had some interesting shots of Adam relaxing at home, chilled out on the sofa, the photos in the café were enthralling. She ran her fingers over the picture of Adam, his head thrown back in joyful laughter as he played pool with Suzy; there was something about this one, something about the glint in his eye, the delight in his face.
"Oh, shit," she sighed "I am in so much trouble."

"I think that one is my favourite." Suzy made her jump as she commented over her shoulder. The photo she was talking about was the same one TJ had been obsessing over. TJ nodded and began shuffling the others around. "So did you get any good shots from the balcony?"
"Suz!" TJ called out, outraged that she would even suggest something like that. "I didn't take any... well I did but... but I didn't keep any."
Suzy just raised her eyebrows. "Alright. You need to start getting ready if you want me to do your hair before work."

"Right. I will be two mins."

Whilst Suzy made her dinner, TJ reached for her camera and began flicking through the numerous shots of Adam at work, with his staff and then at the house. She fell upon the pictures she had lied to Suzy about, the pictures that she just couldn't bring herself to delete. Allowing a soft moan to escape her lips, she slowly scrolled through the shots, Adam pressed against some woman, his hands exploring her, consuming her, now TJ would have to spend the whole evening watching Adam and this woman, knowing they were probably going to do the same thing tonight.

"Aarrgghh, what am I doing?" she called out loud.

"Getting in the shower," Suzy answered for her.

There was no getting out of this, she had basically invited herself so couldn't back out now, she would just have to suck it up and get ready.

Stepping into the shower, she tried desperately to wash away the need that was growing inside her; how had she allowed a man to affect her so much? How had she allowed herself to feel so strongly for someone that obviously had issues? Not to mention a girlfriend! Well, not girlfriend, but a woman in his life he was intimate with! She had only been there to take photographs, her first job since university and she was messing it up big style.

The warm water offered no distraction as she tried to put all her thoughts to the back of her mind, tried to focus on other things. Thoughts of the dogs' home came into her mind, their beautiful yet painful, sad eyes. A tear merged with the water that was streaming down her cheek as she thought once more about Ghost, the poor mistreated dog who could not connect with people. All of a sudden she had a thought, an idea that blossomed and grew inside her mind. Without wasting a second she rushed out of the shower and into her room, she needed to get these ideas down before they left her. Before she had to leave for the party.

Adam gracefully made his way around the room, greeting each guest with a charming smile and a hearty handshake. His mother had really outdone herself this time. The hallway of their simple but large house sparkled and glowed. People wafted from the hall to the lounge and out onto the patio, chatting away pleasantly.

"Thank you for this, Adam."

Adam smiled at his mother affectionately. "Why? This is your event. You have done all the work, Mum."

"Yes, but you are here and that makes it special to me." She left him after giving him a little squeeze on the arm and moved to speak to her friends who had called her over. His gaze was drawn to the doorway, wondering where TJ was, whether she had changed her mind. His jaw dropped as she walked in.

"Hi, I am TJ. I have an invitation." TJ offered the exquisite card over to the suit who stood before her.

After scrutinising her for a while he finally let her in. Her heart raced as she saw endless women all in the most amazing dresses. She stood motionless as they seemed to float from one room to the other, metres of material flourishing around them.

It wasn't long before her eyes fell upon Adam. He had already seen her and was striding over to her purposefully. TJ never usually liked the suit types but seeing Adam was breathtaking. He wore no tie and his shirt was opened a little, the tight-cut suit framed him like a masterpiece. All TJ wanted to do was grab a camera and capture his beauty for all time.

Adam could not get to TJ quick enough. Damn these people for being between them. He liked TJ, she was fun. On their outings he had got to know her pretty well, but tonight he was seeing her in a whole new light. It was the boots he had noticed first, high-heeled, black long boots. They made a unique noise across the marbled hall as though announcing her arrival. His eyes had then grazed over the skin-hugging black jeans. He couldn't help but grin, with all these women here trying to outdo each other in their fancy gowns - TJ had arrived in jeans.

It was then his eyes rose higher and his breath became more rapid. Never had he seen something so pure and delicate, but sexy as hell, all at the same time. One shoulder was draped in a sheer material leaving the other bare; it skimmed over her arm and across her neckline, then fell to barely cover her chest, leaving her torso exposed. The most delicate, fragile, purple butterflies covered her modesty. Adam's imagination soared as he imagined those tiny animals flying away, revealing all. The effect she was having on him was uncontrollable and he felt a mixture of desire and anger as he struggled to gain control. He saw TJ staring at him and the dilemma dissolved as their eyes connected. TJ turned quickly, and seeing the buffet made a beeline straight for it.

"Jeans, really?" Adam's voice whispered into the back of her neck, causing her to gasp a little. "I'm sorry, I didn't mean to startle you."
"You didn't, I just...erm was a bit cold, that's all." Her eyes shot downwards, finding a non-existent spot of dust on her trouser leg. "I know, it was really bad idea, wasn't it. I just thought, I didn't want to look the same as everyone else. You know?"
Adam shook his head. "TJ, you are nothing like anyone else. That outfit definitely makes a statement, believe me, you stand out. I saw you from right across the room." His eyes began to roam again, as the tiny insects drew him in once more. "These are just remarkable, TJ. They are so detailed, are they all handmade?" He reached out to touch one, frightened to break it. Intricate beading edged the wings and each one was painted with an individual pattern. TJ held her breath, unable to take her eyes off him as he studied her. Desperate to change the subject, she blurted out:

"Do you like my little addition?" She pointed to her stomach. Adam saw something glistening in her navel.

"Think I need a closer look," he muttered mischievously.

Panic ensued as TJ was mortified to watch Adam drop to his knees, face level with her stomach. She frantically tried to push him away but he had both hands firmly gripping her waist.

"It's a coffee cup," he called out cheerfully, "Oh my God, TJ, that's so thoughtful, it's beautiful."

"Yes, well. It's just a silly thing; I thought you would find it funny, you being the coffee king and all that. Now please will you get up because people are talking."

Her pleas fell on deaf ears, Adam did not care what anyone else thought, he was trying to hold himself together. This little act, this silly, little act was causing his heart to pound through his ears, his breath was heavy and he could not move. TJ's horror became complete when Adam's father joined them.

"Any chance you could remove your face from that young lady's crotch, son?" he joked. TJ's face was now matching her butterflies' colour as she stood, humiliated.

"Look, Dad," Adam muttered, "Look what TJ's wearing."

"Yes, not a lot. I had noticed, your mother gave me a good slap on the arm for noticing." He winked playfully at TJ.

"No, there!" He pointed at her stomach. Adam's father reached into his jacket and pulled out a pair of spectacles. Balancing them on his nose, he too knelt down to gaze.

"Well, would you look at that. Isn't that lovely."

TJ's nightmare was now complete as both father and son gazed at her belly button jewel; she closed her eyes tightly and balled her hands into fists praying it would end, wishing she had never had the stupid idea.

Her prayers were answered by Adam's mother.

"Get up now, you two, for goodness sake. The pair of you are embarrassing yourselves, not to mention poor Jem. Come on, why don't we pop outside for a moment whilst these two compose themselves."

Relief washed over TJ as the woman guided her by the arm and threw a disgusted huff over her shoulder at the pair of men still kneeling on the floor.

"You may have to help me up, son."

Adam chuckled as he grabbed his father's arm and hauled him up to standing, all sorts of strange noises leaving his father's lips as he did so.

Chapter 10

THE REFRESHING, NIGHT AIR calmed down TJ's glowing face and she let a sigh of relief escape. The gardens of the house were breathtaking. Exquisite and tasteful but at the same time they had a family feel to them. Large grassy areas were surrounded by colourful borders, stacked with flowers and shrubs. There was a wooded area at the far of the garden that TJ imagined was an amazing place to grow up, a kid's paradise with places to hide and trees to climb.

Barbara watched her as she gazed at her own personal retreat. This was the place Barbara went to sort out all her problems, where she made all her big decisions in life.

"So what do you think?" she asked TJ.
"Wow, Barbara. I mean it is just breathtakingly beautiful, I could spend my whole life taking pictures here."

Barbara just smiled. "I meant about my son!" she corrected sternly. TJ turned, aghast she would ask such a question. The expression on her face told Barbara everything she needed to know. No way was TJ about to start talking about her feelings for Adam to his mother. She had not even made a decision herself about how she felt, well, she knew how she felt but was unsure as to how to proceed, or if she should proceed.

"Alright, alright, I get it. Adam is a no go topic." Barbara chuckled to herself. TJ did not need to answer the question, she had all the answers she needed from the one look of horror TJ had displayed. Now she just had to work on her stubborn son.

They began to slowly walk towards the trees, all the while gentle breezes presented opportunities for TJ to view the garden differently. A waving branch, blossom falling, even birds in the bushes created new sounds, different shadows cast upon the immaculate lawn.

It took a small sob from Barbara for TJ to wake up from her daydream; the woman's face was pale and her eyes glistened as tears formed. TJ felt awkward and turned away, not knowing what to say or what had upset her so much.

"I'm sorry, I love my garden and there are so many happy memories here. My son, my other son, Brian, planted all these for me. Not here of course, we did not live in such grandeur when the boys were little. But I had them moved here when Adam bought this place for us." TJ remembered Adam talking about his older brother and suddenly felt like she was also grieving for him, a lump developed in her throat. "Oh please, don't let me upset you." Barbara threw her arms around TJ, pulling her to her chest.

The two women stood for a while, bathed in moonlight, holding each other, consoling each other, before Barbara finally pulled away. "Come on, we had better head in."
"What was Brian like?" TJ asked tentatively, "I mean, Adam told me a little about him ... about ... how he died."

Barbara's eyes widened. Adam had never spoken about Brian to anyone before, let alone a woman. She suddenly realised that the little glimmer of hope she had, that Adam and TJ might get together, was obviously closer to happening than she had first thought. She had longed for her son to find someone, to have love in his life. Adam had different ideas, for years he had thrown himself into the cafés, not allowing himself a real, genuine social life. TJ, it seemed, had actually managed to get him to open up, and if Adam had spoken to her about Brian, she did not feel any reason for her not to.

"You don't have to," TJ interjected quickly, seeing the hesitation.

"I think that would be nice."

She linked her arm through TJ's. "Brian was a wild thing," she grinned, gazing off into the distance, "Not like Adam. Adam was just a ball of rage from the day he was born, used to scream for hours! No, Brian was charming, he was all smiles and big eyes, then two minutes later you would find out that he had skipped school for three days." She held TJ's hand tightly, enjoying the chance to share her memories with someone.

Adam desperately searched the crowd of faces, needing to see TJ's peering back at him. He knew his mother had taken her from him but now it had been over half an hour and he could see neither of them. Finally he released the breath he had unconsciously been holding as his mother appeared, TJ trailing behind.

"She really is a beautiful young woman, Adam." His father's hand slapped him on the shoulder, making him jump. "I do hope you're going to try to hold onto this one and not scare her away!"

"Dad!" Adam cried out, aghast, "...she's not mine to hold onto." But even as the words spilled out of him, he knew how much he wanted to change that.

"They are useless," Barbara declared to TJ as they came closer. "Take him for example," she said, waving her hand in her husband's general direction. "I ask him his opinion on these earrings and what do I get? ...Well, what I get is 'Are they new?' New! Let me tell you, dear, he bought me these for our tenth anniversary and he doesn't even remember."

TJ stared wide-eyed at the man, "Really! Mr M, that is so bang out of order." Derek smirked at the fake scolding.
"That's not true, I was just playing, Babs," he protested.
She threw him a stern 'whatever' look and shook her head to Adam and TJ, but Derek had not finished.
"If that was the case, sweetheart, how on earth would I know to buy this for you?" He reached into his jacket pocket and pulled out a beautiful string of exquisite, pink pearls.

The exact match for her earrings.

"Oh, Dad, that was smooth." Adam high-fived him as he watched his mother fill up and clutch her heart. "Come on, TJ, we had better leave these two, they have gone into the 'zone'."

TJ watched just a moment longer, unable to keep the smile from her face as Derek and Barbara gazed at each other, no words needing to be spoken. It was a moment TJ would have loved to capture with her camera. Christ, she felt naked without it.

It was the wrong side of two in the morning before TJ left the Morgans' house. It had been a night of laughter, tears and some amazing goodwill. She had expected to feel out of place, a lump of coal in a tray of diamonds.

When she had first walked in, in just her jeans, she had felt everyone stare, but now, leaving, she felt like she had a new circle of friends. She reminisced about all the people she had met, the stories she had been told about losing loved ones, or stories of remarkable recovery. Adam's mother, Barbara, certainly had a strong presence in the community and expected everyone to help out, not just throw money at a party but volunteer time and ideas. She did not participate in charity for appearances; she wanted to help, to make a difference. She was an inspirational woman.

The lights flashed by as the taxi sped towards TJ's flat, the early morning air still warm and welcoming. Tinges of orange began to highlight the skyline as dawn tried to push away the weighty night skies. Thoughts drifted back to Adam, his beauty and presence as he had strode over to her. His grace with his mother and the respect and love she felt from them both. She knew Adam was dangerously handsome but this gentle side of him she had not expected. First the shock of the dogs' home, then the protective concern at the party. TJ was falling hard.

Had fallen hard.

"Shit, screw this," she muttered to herself.

"Sorry? This turn, did you say?" the taxi driver called out from behind his protective glass barrier.

"No, no. Just talking to myself. Keep going until you get to the junction."

Chapter 11

THE DAYS BEFORE THE EXHIBITION had painfully dragged by. TJ had all the photos blown up into various sizes and had spent hours deciding exactly how she wanted them to be displayed. She had arranged the displays, created mood lighting, mixed a good array of serious and joyful images. Every day surrounded by Adam's face. Every day having to choose from hundreds of variations of his face, trying to match up Barbara's requests with the image she wanted to portray. Now that everything was almost done, a new fear had gripped her.

Adam was going to hate this.

"Adam, I swear to the gods of wind and fire if you don't change your face I am going to change it for you!" Derek stood in the doorway whilst his son sighed at the reflection in his mirror.
"Why did she have to do this, Dad? I mean the last thing I want is to go and see a load of pictures of me!" The tie he was attempting to secure tangled

round his fingers one more time, and he viciously ripped it off and threw it on the floor. "Fucking thing!" he ranted.

"Wow, there's the old Adam we all know and love." Derek moved across the room and after retrieving the tie, beckoned his son to stand up. "Now, son. Your mother wants this. She firmly believes that it will help your business."

"Hah!" Adam spit out. "Yeah, they are gonna see a stupid, arsehole screaming at his staff."

"They will see no such thing," Barbara called out from the hallway. "I have total faith that Jem will have captured some fantastic images of the real you. Now get your backside into that car."

Adam groaned and with his head hung low, left the comfort of his house and reluctantly sat in the car. The rage within him grew and grew as the street lights whizzed by. He could feel heat radiating off him the more annoyed he became. Why couldn't his mother just stay out of his business? Why did she always have to stick her nose in? He rubbed his forehead, trying to calm himself down, suddenly wishing he had his old bands on his wrist so that he could distract himself from the dread that filled him.

He was so consumed with his own misery that he didn't notice they had reached the gallery. His mother and father were already out of the car and waiting for him. Derek knocked on the window, shaking Adam out of his trance.

"When you are ready, son?" His father now opened the door for him, leaving him nowhere to run.

"For God's sake, Adam, it's a few pictures," his mother scorned. "Suck it up and deal with it! You might like what you see."

The gallery owner greeted them as they entered, shaking each one's hands in an over-enthusiastic welcome. Adam grunted a greeting of sorts, refusing to lift his eyes from the floor. The minute he straightened up, he would see his face. His face everywhere. The pit of his stomach felt inflamed, the voices of his mother and father drowned out as the fury flowed through to his ears, muffling all the sounds around him.

He knew he would have to look up at some point, surely TJ would not embarrass him, they had shared a few wonderful days and he had really felt a connection with her. Maybe she was just being nice to get her pictures, after all her reputation was on the line. But then images of her asleep flooded his thoughts. Watching her on his balcony, sighing, murmuring his name – God, she had sounded so sexy. A calmness began to soothe him and he felt his temperature fall a little.

With his thoughts overflowing with TJ, he lifted his head prepared for the sight that would greet him, only it wasn't his face that he saw. His viewpoint went straight into the eyes of his beloved Bulldog, his head tilted and large pink tongue flopping to the side. Adam smiled and reached out to touch the picture.

"She has a real talent, that girl of yours." A familiar voice spoke behind him making him jump.

Malika stood grinning at the picture with him; she nodded her head at some of the other work. Glancing around the exhibit, he saw pictures of himself everywhere, but no one was looking at him. In between his portraits were the most emotional pictures of all the dogs in the home. On closer inspection he could see that their story had been written down also. People had hands clasped over their mouths as they read the tragic stories, or were joyously giggling at the pictures of the puppies.

"She came back," Malika explained. "Asked if I minded her taking some pictures. Adam, she spent all day listening to the stories." She smiled a knowing smile and placed a hand on his shoulder. "I like her," she added, as though he needed her approval.

Adam remained silent. A confused frown on his face. How could she do this? How had she done this? He had been dreading this, fearful that people would judge him, see him for the uneducated man he was. They would laugh, whisper behind his back that he was a joke. All his deep, dark fears had been awakened. But no one was whispering, and no one was looking at his pictures and it was all down to TJ.

His heart began to pound, the conflict of emotions tormenting him. On the one hand, TJ had taken all the attention away from him; she had turned the whole event around, understood how he was feeling. On the other hand, she had taken the one thing that was private to him, personal, and splashed it all over the walls for everyone to see. His sanctuary had been declared public. He slowly released his breath and it escaped with a shaky noise. It was then he saw her. Nervously scanning the room, she stood in a tight black dress, her legs elongated by high heels. His blood once again began to boil.

Now she decides to wear a dress, he thought.

"Oh, shit." TJ saw Adam thundering towards her, his mouth pulled into a tight line, his eyebrows scrunched together.

 He looked livid.

"Talk. In private. Now!" Adam hissed. TJ pointed to the office then gasped as Adam grabbed her arm and practically dragged her in there.
"I know what you are going to say." TJ tried to justify her actions as she turned to face him. He had his back to her, his hand on the door handle, his forehead pressed against the closed door.

She had no idea he would be this mad, she thought he might be a little pissed off with her, but she had hoped that he would understand why. She had been told that Adam had a temper, right now she didn't need to see his face to know he was mad.

"Why?" he breathed.
"I wanted to make you feel better, your mum wanted your pictures on display, you didn't want to be seen," she blurted out, her words merging into one. "I thought it would be the best of both worlds, I have not mentioned that you have anything to do with the dogs' home, there are no images of you there or with any of the dogs. As far as anyone knows we are just fund-raising at the same time."

She dragged a breath, wishing she could go outside for some cool, night air. The air in the office felt hot and suffocating. "Adam, I don't need this. I did my job, now if you will move I can get on with it." TJ charged for the door, trying to wrestle the handle from Adam. He was quicker. Grabbing her, he spun her round so that her back was now firmly thrown against the door. Adam stood like a formidable force in front of her, darkness in his eyes as his stared.
"Shut up," Adam growled, and before TJ could utter another word Adam's mouth clamped down on hers. For a second she was motionless, shocked by his actions. It didn't take long for her body to catch up.

He was merciless. She grasped his head between her hands in an attempt to slow him down but he responded by grabbing her wrists and pinning them to the door. TJ gasped, the passion, the need of the man overwhelmed her. Her skin was on fire, every inch of her body cried out for him. She turned her head, desperate to catch her breath. Adam continued his assault, biting her neck, unable to get close enough to her. His body pressed her hard into the door but she hardly noticed. An animalistic need blurring her brain, the room spinning so hard she screwed up her eyes to make it stop. Christ, if this is what happened every time she pissed him off, she would remember to do it more often.

Without warning Adam pulled at her knee, making her wrap her leg round his waist. A growl escaped his lips and his eyes closed, as though fighting with himself. Hell no, TJ was not about to let him talk himself out of this. This was no time for logic or reason. She held onto the door handle and hoisted her other leg around his waist, mimicking what she had seen through the window that night. She reached into his back pocket and pulled out his wallet. *Please God, let there be a foil packet in here*, she prayed.

His eyes bore into her as she threw the disregarded wallet aside and ripped into the packet. Slowly, he lowered her legs to allow her to cover him, his breathing was heavy and she knew he was using every ounce of strength to control himself. She wasted no time, as soon as he was sheathed; her legs resumed their place, pulling him to her. He lost the fight and lifting her skirt; he ripped her pants to the side and entered her in one stroke.

TJ nearly screamed as he filled her, her body alive and so sensitive. No words were spoken. He barely looked at her again but TJ was too consumed to care. Never had she known that he could be like this, so free, so wild. Her nails dug into the back of his head as she pulled his hair, trying to keep herself from flying apart. With one last thrust, TJ surrendered, sinking her teeth into his shoulder to keep herself quiet. Adam remained motionless, his fingers digging into her thighs.

When TJ was sure her legs would hold her weight, she released her grip on Adam and tentatively stood up. That was the first time Adam made eye contact with her, his face did not reflect her own. Whilst she was flushed, her cheeks rosy and a contented smile on her face, Adam's remained stern and grey. Without a word he adjusted himself and left, not once looking back.

Chapter 12

ADAM COULD NOT GET out of there quick enough; what the hell had he done? He had practically assaulted the first girl he had cared about for years. His mind raced as he hailed a taxi, there was only one place he could go to.

"Jesus Christ," Robert uttered as he opened the door to a dishevelled Adam. "Come in. Talk to me."

Robert Millarson had known Adam for years; they had met at school and become firm friends. Adam knew university was not for him but had pushed Robert to go. When Robert's mother had died, shortly followed by his father's death, Adam had kept Robert sane, making him manager of The Coffee Café. He gave him a focus, stopped him spiralling out of control. He now dealt with everything to do with Adam's baby, the flagship café that started it all off.

Adam went to the bathroom to wash his face and relieve himself of the condom that remained. A token of his disgraceful behaviour. He grimaced at his face in the mirror.

"I've really fucked up this time!"

A few beers later Adam began to tell Robert the whole story, how he met TJ, finding her asleep on the balcony, then the events of the evening.

"Holy shit!" Robert admired. "Right there in the office, with all those people outside! You have some balls, man." He chuckled, opening another beer.

"It's not funny, Robert!" Adam complained. "I don't think I even spoke to her, didn't say a word to her. She is gonna think I am some monster, an animal. I acted like a total bastard."

He drained his beer and slammed it onto the table.

"Calm down. Don't wreck my furniture over it." Robert wiped the glass table, checking for damage. Satisfied that it was intact, he turned to Adam again.

"Right. Let's look at this objectively. Did she push you away? Give you any sign that she didn't want you to do it?"

Adam vaguely remembered her pushing him off and he buried his head in his hands. "Shit, what have I done?"

"Okay, let's try another one. Who instigated it?" Robert tried again.

"Who the FUCK do you think instigated it?" Adam roared, standing up to face off with Robert.

Robert, however, remained seated, more than used to his friend's outbursts. He raised his eyebrows at Adam, waiting for him to sit down again. Adam's mind was a blur, he had been so angry at her, so violated that she had invaded his privacy- had he now violated her? He was so confused, unable to remember the details. But on the other hand she had done it so gracefully, so full of care that he had just wanted to show her, there and then, how much it meant to him.

"Well?" Robert persisted.
"She took out my wallet to get a condom," he muttered, the fog lifting a little. He had had his eyes closed most of the time but an image of TJ's face flooded his thoughts. So sexy, so aroused. How the hell could she have been aroused when he had been such a monster?
"Oh, there you go then," Robert said triumphantly, throwing a handful of peanuts into his mouth. Adam, however, was not convinced. How had he allowed himself to get into that state again? He vowed he would always keep control, but the torrent of different emotions he felt that night had pushed him over the edge.

Something he was NEVER going to do again.

It was TJ's turn to feel pissed off. How dare Adam just walk out the door? He had just given her the most explosive orgasm she had ever had, and then just left. She had sat in the office, trying to calm herself down for over half an hour before she summoned the courage to go back out there. Barbara was the first person to speak to her.

"Jem, I am so sorry. Did Adam have a go at you? Was he cross? I am disgusted with him. He has stormed out of here and left everyone, all his business contacts are wondering what the hell has happened." She wiped a stray tear that had fallen from TJ's eye. "I am so, so sorry, my dear. Really I am. I am gonna KILL him when I get to him." She embraced TJ affectionately. Little did she know that TJ's tears were born from frustration, not from being distressed.

The rest of the evening went without a hitch. Everyone seemed happy with her work, a few people had asked for her business card. But what was more wonderful, was that Malika had made several appointments with people who wanted to meet some of the dogs. Even Ghost. She wished Adam was there to hear the news but she, of all people, knew how tempers could take over a person. She understood why he was mad, she also knew in time he would thank her for what she had done. How long that would take? Who knew?

It was past midnight before TJ finally managed to climb into her bed, the cool sheets offering a wonderful release. She played over in her mind everything that had happened. Adam had already, unknowingly, wormed himself into her heart; she knew that the day they went to the rescue centre together. He had such a beautiful caring side, she felt like she was seeing something no one else got to see, like he was offering a piece of himself to her. But tonight, tonight her body had loved him, finally understanding what her heart was talking about. His eyes had been dark, scary almost. She knew he was fighting to keep control but instead of helping him relax, she had encouraged the monster to surface. Her body began to respond to the memory of him, her breath rasped as the memory almost had her reaching dizzy heights again. How was she going to deal with this? Should she approach him? Or wait for him to come to her?

The alarm clock brought TJ out of the most wonderful dream, a dream that she had been having all night. She smiled and rolled over to see a card propped up against her bedside lamp. Rubbing her eyes, she saw a note from Suzy.

This came for you this morning. Had to go to work. Hope last night went well, I want all the details tonight.

Love ya

Suz

xx

The envelope had been hand delivered; no address was written on it. She sat up, ripping it open, a small note fell out. It simply said:

Thank you and I am sorry.
Adam

Thank you for what? she pondered. *Thank you for the photos or the sex?*

There was a card with the note, a gift certificate. It stated that as a thank you she could choose any dog to adopt - subject to Malika's approval - and all costs and vet bills would be taken care of.

Adam knew TJ was desperate for a dog; they had talked about it when she had stayed with him. Her heart leapt at this thoughtful gesture; however the note had showed that he felt ashamed of what had happened. He was sorry. TJ decided she would have to put him straight on that. If anyone understood about the monster within, it was her.

She embraced it, whilst Adam hid it.

That needed to change.

Showering and changing, she decided she would have to deviate a little from her planned day. She was supposed to be finding a new flat, as she was a student no more; she needed to move out of the digs she shared with Suzy. Suzy had agreed to help her decorate and she was really excited about living on her own, but now she felt scared. She didn't want to go alone, and she knew just the person to accompany her.

"Adam, you have a visitor." Anthony, his assistant, buzzed.
"Not in the mood, Ant. Send them away!" Adam snapped as he tried to focus on the list of figures in front of him.
"Might be a bit difficult," Anthony gingerly replied.
"And why is that, Anthony?"

"Because she has already barged her way in!" TJ snarled as his office door swung wide open. She stood there, her hands on her hips, her beautiful breasts rising and falling with each agitated breath. Breasts that he still had not seen, had not been allowed to worship in his haste to have her.
 A very timid man stood behind her.
"I am sorry, Adam.... she just..."
"It's fine, Ant, go on, I will deal with her." Anthony nodded his head and began to leave. "Oh, Ants, will you try and rearrange my next appointment please?" he asked.
"If you are doing that, can you rearrange his whole afternoon please? Thanks," TJ commanded before closing the door on him.
"I can't just change all my appointments, TJ!" he huffed, dreading the argument that was bound to ensue. "Before you start, I am sorry....I just...."

TJ did not allow him to finish, "You can stop right there before you start all your self-pity crap!" She ran her fingers through her hair, shaking it slightly with an air of confidence. "I need someone to come flat hunting with me."

"And you came to ask me?" Adam asked puzzled. This was not going at all the way he thought it would.

"No, I didn't come to ask you. I came to tell you. Sort out your appointments." She moved to sit in a chair across the room. "Come on, hurry up!"

Adam sat aghast; what the hell? How dare she just come into his workplace and rearrange his day? He had apologised for last night, sent her a card and gift and she had not even mentioned it, just made demands. As cross as he tried to be he couldn't help feeling relieved that she was still talking to him, that she hadn't screamed at him and told him she never wanted to see him again.

"I am sorry, TJ." He tried again to apologise.

"Well I am not, so get over it!"

Her reply shocked him and his reaction coaxed a sly smile from her. The intercom buzz made him jump, tearing his eyes away from her he answered.

"All your appointments have been moved, which means that you are free for today and tomorrow morning - just in case." The sarcastic tone in Anthony's voice did not escape Adam.

"Well, that's all sorted then," TJ said, rising to her feet. "Come on, then." She left, waving to Anthony as she passed him, not waiting for Adam to catch up.

"I like her!" Anthony whispered as Adam finally got himself together and left.
"Shut up!" Adam replied, but Anthony just laughed.

Adam had no social life; he certainly never had any women in his office. He just worked and as far as Anthony knew, never had anyone close. Yet this woman had invited herself here, given instructions to his staff and Adam had allowed her to do this. It was a unique event that the office gossips would dine out on for weeks, Anthony being one of them. He loved his boss but this was too juicy to hold in, so he picked up the phone and began dialling.

129 Distinct Desire

Chapter 13

ADAM COMPLAINED AS THEY stood outside yet another apartment. The sunlight burned his eyes and he dug around in his pocket to find his sunglasses. They had been at this for most of the day and other than a quick sandwich break, had not stopped.

TJ was hard to please, not that the sort of apartments she could afford were luxurious, but she had a picture in her mind and none of them were matching up to it.

"Don't look so miserable!" she chided. "This is the last one."

Adam responded with a bored glare before following her up the steps to a slimy, greasy-haired man who dangled a key in front of him.

"You will love this place, Miss Knapley, I promise you!" he smarmed.

"Really?" She questioned, "...and how exactly do you know what I will and will not like? Are you dictating to me that I will like it? I don't respond to that!" And with a swish of her hair she marched herself back down the steps without putting as much as a toe inside. Adam sucked in his top lip, stifling a laugh. God, she had balls, nothing fazed her. She felt no obligation to be polite or respectful to anyone who didn't deserve it.

He was so jealous of her for that.

"Right, I guess I have put you through enough, come on, let's go get a drink." TJ linked her arm through his, dragging him off.

"No." Adam stopped suddenly. "I am done letting you dictate everything today. I want a shower, a nice home-cooked meal and some beers from my own fridge." His eyes stared defiantly into her own. "You are invited, of course," he added quickly, fearing he had given the wrong impression.

"For which part?" She tilted her head slightly and widened her eyes, daring him to answer. He just smiled and continued walking to the road, and hailing a taxi he opened the passenger door and took a step back. She hesitated for a while then dived in, just like she knew she would.

It felt different somehow, entering Adam's apartment this time. She felt on edge, almost nervous.

"I need to catch up with the office, see what I missed if that's alright with you?"

TJ nodded as she moved over to gaze out of the window, as memories of her night out on the balcony came flooding back to her.

"You are welcome to use the shower if you like, there are some spare clothes in the cupboard, dressing gowns and ..." His words trailed off as he became absorbed in his phone, tapping away on the screen, muttering away to himself as he walked to his office.

Why not? TJ thought. She moved to the adjoining door, only to discover it was locked. If she couldn't use that room, she would have to use his. Unsure, she made her way up the stairs to his bathroom. There were three doors upstairs, all open, and unwilling to resist she glanced into each one. The first room was a stark white room, it had a running machine and some other equipment in, and a large TV loomed from the far wall. The second was the bathroom; without really caring, she moved on. Her heart raced as she moved towards what must be Adam's bedroom, she felt disgusting, invading his privacy like this but at the same time was curious to see.

"One door too far, Tabby Cat." TJ froze in her tracks as Adam's deep voice reverberated down the hall. "You know, if you wanted to see my bedroom, you just had to ask," he continued, reaching past her as he pushed the door wide open, allowing her entrance.

"I'm sorry; I don't know what's wrong with me sometimes. I didn't mean to...."
Adam silenced her with a brief kiss, it lasted just a second but it was enough to set TJ alight. "Don't apologise; you were going to see it at some point tonight." His smile made her toes curl and her head began to swim. Adam strolled into the room and perched on the end of the bed. "Does it meet your high standards, Tabby Cat?"

TJ hadn't even seen the room, all she could see was the delicious man before her, his eyes twinkling in that mysterious way.
"You catch up with all your work then?" she teased as she seductively swayed over to him. He licked his lips like a predator about to devour his prey. TJ was the most sexy, unusual woman he had ever met; the need for her had gone way beyond physical. He had taken what he wanted and she had come back to him, not shunned him or sent him away. Tonight he would show her how much she meant to him.

TJ sulked as the water beat her back, she had offered herself to him, stood before him and all he had done was walk away. How dare he? What the hell was wrong with him? The tension in her built by the second as her head was filled with all the things she had wanted to do.
"Shit!" she sighed. This guy had her in tatters, she thought a few nights with him might get him out of her system, but now she realised it was not going to be that easy.

She had never felt this strongly for someone, anyone. Men came and went in her life, sometimes they stayed a while, sometimes just for the night, but Adam, Adam was different. She was playing with him, and he was playing back. The teasing had her all knotted up, at least that was one thing she could sort out on her own.

Snuggling into the large dressing gown she headed off to find Adam, now relaxed and glowing she felt her confidence increasing, he couldn't say no to her now. Hearing noise in the kitchen she opened the door only to find a woman in there.

"Oh, sorry," TJ gasped, wrapping the towel gown tighter around herself. The woman looked just as shocked to see TJ, as she was to see her.
"Are you supposed to be here?" the woman asked, standoffish.
"Yes!" bit TJ, "I'm here with Adam." How dare she speak to her like that, TJ thought. "I'm TJ; check it with his lordship if you like!"
The woman's face suddenly changed and a smile appeared across her cracked wrinkled face.
"So you're TJ."

The woman had embraced TJ warmly, much to her annoyance. She was a short woman, probably in her fifties or so, her hair was black and short, framing her formidable face.

She made TJ a coffee and introduced herself. It seemed that she had been a neighbour of his family and would babysit for them when needed; she had grown very fond of Adam and had been very proud of watching his growing success.

"So you still babysit him now?" TJ joked.

"Sort of," she replied. "Adam has helped a lot of people round here, you know. He offered jobs, employed his friends, family, neighbours. I used to do bits of cleaning in the cafés but now I just help him out here. He has precious little time for cleaning and shopping." Her eyes showed great affection as she talked, and TJ felt drawn to her.

"Oh shit, Maggie, I didn't know you were in today?" Adam was flustered, his eyes moving between the two women.

"Clearly!" Maggie said sarcastically, staring straight at him. "I only came to drop some shopping off, make sure you were eating properly." She closed the fridge and picked up her handbag. "I will be off then, nice to meet you, dear." She patted TJ on the shoulder as she left.

"She seems nice." TJ turned to Adam, who now had his head in his hands.

"I give it five minutes," he muttered. It did not take that long. Within seconds his phone was ringing. "Hey, Mum," he answered without even checking his screen. TJ sniggered. Maggie had obviously called her immediately after closing the front door.

"No, I'm..... no....Mum, I am not. Yes, it's TJ." He held the handset away from his ear and rolled his eyes, sighing heavily. "Mum! Give me a break. I will talk to you tomorrow...... What? .....No I am not asking her.....but....but....FINE!!!" He ended the call. "You've been invited to a barbeque."

"Nice, tell her thank you." TJ laughed. Adam narrowed his eyes towards her and muttered something about the women in his life.

TJ followed him into the lounge area, "So have you finished all your work now?" she asked him suggestively.

"Yes, all caught up, no thanks to you." His voice lowered, sending heat coursing through her.

"Mmm, what could we do now?" She played with her robe ties. Adam was aware of what she was doing but his eyes never left hers.

"I can tell you one thing." He stood up to face her, "We are not doing what we did the other night!" Disappointment flooded her, she had thought of nothing else but that night.

Adam slid his hand into hers and began to lead her up the stairs.

"This time we go slowly!"

Chapter 14

TJ AWOKE AND STRETCHED OUT, elongating every bone in her body. Her muscles were all relaxed and warm after their vigorous workout. She had to admit that as much as she enjoyed the excitement of an angry Adam, gentle sex was pretty amazing. Her whole body hummed in contentment.

Adam's head popped round the door, rousing her from her daydream. "You're awake, are you?" he chirped. "Thought I had finished you off for good." His playful little smile made her bite down a retort and she pulled herself to a seated position. Adam froze in the doorway as the sheet delicately slid down her body, gathering at her waist, allowing him a glorious view of her breasts. Those delicious round, firm breasts. His body was beginning to react and damn it, if she didn't notice. Why did everything feel like a competition with this woman?

"Come on, Tabby Cat. Breakfast time," he commanded, desperate to gain a little control of the situation.

"Sounds perfect," she replied dreamily, gliding out of the bed and swaying into the bathroom. His eyes watched every move, every contour of her body. Every single wrinkle in her backside as she walked. His heart now pounded, his body screaming at him to follow her, almost pointing him in her direction. "Not again," he muttered. He was not about to follow her around like some horny little puppy. She did not make all his decisions for him.

Not this time.

"Bastard." TJ had stood waiting in the bathroom, adamant that he would follow her. She had watched his eyes blacken as the sheet fell; his tongue almost hanging out as she walked past him. So, WHERE THE HELL WAS HE? Her body felt all tight and aching again. She hated the impact Adam was having on her, she yearned for him, desired him but he just wasn't playing it her way. That really pissed her off. Not bothering to dress, she grabbed a t-shirt from his dresser and stomped downstairs.

Adam was banging things around in the kitchen. "Fuck it!" he yelled out as he spilt coffee over the side. Turning to grab a cloth, he saw TJ as she reached the last stair. The sight of her in his top broke his very last resolve. Clear thinking was no longer an option; he had been trying to get images of

TJ out of his mind. Unfortunately in doing so all he had done was think about her more, his erection now so prominent, it was painful.

Then he saw her. His eyes clouded, his brain fogged over and he almost growled. He was losing it, losing control. They had just spent an amazing night together, he had never had a woman spend the night at his home, but with TJ, he hadn't thought twice about it. They had bonded with each other, loved each other. TJ had screamed his name, begging him to allow her release, raising her up so high and then, only when he was ready, did he finally allow her to fly apart.

But he was now losing the battle.

Oh, crap, TJ thought, *what have I done now?* Adam was just standing, staring. His body was rigid like a marbled statue. But before she had time to question him, Adam had her. She hadn't even noticed him cross the room; he must have been like lightning. His mouth was on hers, taking her questions and her breath.

In one swift move TJ found herself bent over the back of the sofa, Adam inside her. She gasped as she fought to catch her breath, unable and unwilling to speak. Wave after wave of pleasure surged through her, her arms aching as she tried to brace herself against the assault. She could not see Adam's face nor did she want to. She did not care about his pleasure, only hers. This was carnal, she needed the monster.

Adam cried out as he finally found bliss. TJ's legs gave way and she trembled, falling to a kneeling position. Both panted, unable to speak, exhausted by the sudden rush. Unable to face her, Adam stepped back slowly, his eyes searching for something, anything familiar to bring him back into the world he knew. TJ reached out behind her and held his ankle, gently stroking it, soothing him. Immediately his mind cleared.

"TJ?" He buried his hand into her hair, as he did, she turned. She was beautiful, her skin was pink and roses flourished on her cheeks. Her eyes embraced him and her lips, so red and plump invited him in. Gently, he scooped her up into his arms and laid her down on the sofa. As he knelt beside her on the floor, his hand once more dived into the comfort of her golden hair. Both just smiled at one another, Adam massaging TJ's head as her hair threaded through his fingers.

"Adam, I just...Oh, shit...sorry!" Maggie walked in on a scene from a comedy movie. TJ launched herself behind the curtains; Adam futilely tried to cover himself with cushions, cursing her for coming in without warning. Maggie tried to look anywhere but at the two, dropped a bag onto the floor and turned around. "I ... I picked up your clean washing," she announced before rushing out of the door, giggling like a child.

Adam shut his eyes tight, praying that didn't just happen. TJ slowly appeared from behind the curtains; embarrassment didn't sit well with TJ, nothing usually bothered her, but this! A noise broke the very uncomfortable silence. Adam turned to TJ and they both laughed as Adam's ring tone sang out, announcing that his mother had been notified.
"Are you going to answer it?" TJ laughed.
"The humiliation will never end if I don't." Adam sighed aloud as he pressed 'answer'.

TJ did not need to hear the other side of the conversation to know what was being said. Adams face was slowly changing colour, like skin in the scorching midday sun, it became redder and redder as he stood silently listening to his mother. Without thinking, TJ joined him at his side and took his hand in hers, quietly offering support. This inconsequential act suddenly felt like a massive offering, her eyes stared at their hands entwined. She felt a jolt through her, a stabbing in her heart. Her fingers locked around his and she doubted that a crowbar would be able to prise them apart. Adam's voice melted into her ears, making her raise her eye line to his. His face was no longer red, it was almost glowing.

"Mum, enough already. I will bring her and you can ask her yourself, prove I haven't done anything awful to her." He winked at this part and TJ felt her insides churning. "Yes, she is the first, Mum... yes I am being careful...no I have no idea what I am doing." This made TJ chuckle as she imagined Barbara tearing a strip off her son. Once again their eyes locked as Adam finished off the call with, "Yes, I think I am," then ending the call.

"Yes you are what?" she asked him, sensing that she already knew the answer.

"Yes, I think I am falling in love."

"Anyone I know?" she teased.

He didn't dignify her question with a reply.

Adam returned to the kitchen, having slipped his jeans back on and continued with making breakfast. TJ pulled the retrieved shirt back over her head.
Holy shit, she thought, w*hat the hell is happening*?

As she hauled herself onto a stool at the breakfast bar, the smell exuding from the kitchen caused her stomach to growl. All this sex and no food was not a good combination. Adam presented a plate to her with eggs, bacon and pancakes on the side. Filling a plate of his own, he moved round the counter to sit next to her.

"Oh my God, this is sooo good," TJ commended through a mouthful of food. More balanced on her fork ready for the next available space. Scoop after scoop disappeared and gradually her appetite subsided. She was hardly aware of Adam sitting next to her, watching in amazement as this delicate little thing devoured a breakfast large enough to feed a horse.

When she had finally had her fill, she placed down a fork and still staring at the empty plate said, "Are we going to talk about what you said to your mum?"

Adam chuckled, never before had he seen the great and confident TJ seem so small and timid. "Sure," he began, "...there is a barbeque tonight and Mum wants you to come, it's her pre-birthday."

"What the hell is a 'pre-birthday'?" she asked, distracted.

"She has a big bash on her birthday every year, so she likes to have a little get together with family the week before. Just a few friends pop in as well, quite intimate."

TJ was flattered, 'just family' Adam had said. Is that how Barbara saw her? Once again softness enveloped her; she had always been very defensive with people. She was such a loud, boisterous woman; most people did not want to get close to her. She was always prepared; never let anyone get too close. She had let Carla into her life and she had just left her without saying goodbye.

But Adam and his family were different, they had liked her immediately, understood her. Had Adam really meant it when he said he loved her? He was standing at the sink washing the plates, she chuckled as she remembered the space-age dishwasher underneath and wondered if he even knew he had one.

Throwing the dishcloth on the side, he turned and leant over the counter, placing his soft lips against hers. She knew he was waiting for her to say something. Words failed her; she wasn't ready to admit such a big thing to herself, let alone him. Did she love him? So soon? It was a ridiculous thought.

"Come on, Tabby Cat," Adam coaxed playfully. At hearing her nickname she let go of her worries.
"You did only say that you 'thought' you were falling in love with me. I mean that's not exactly concrete, is it?" She folded her arms over her chest. "I mean today you 'think' you do, tomorrow you might 'think' you don't!"
Adam roared with laughter. "Maybe you should make a bit more effort to persuade me." He left her at the counter and moved upstairs.

She knew he was baiting her, making her follow him. She stood, and then sat again trying to decide what to do. Hearing the water in the shower made her realise he was not waiting for her.

Damn him, for making her feel like this!

Damn him, for thinking that she would do exactly what he wanted!

Damn her, for bloody doing it!

Chapter 15

TJ STORMED AROUND HER apartment, her mood not improving despite various attempts to calm. Adam had her in his grasp; he had her bowing to his commands like a lovesick teenager. Never, had she been like this with a man, NEVER.

After showering and dressing in Adam's apartment, she had returned to her own place to get ready for Barbara's birthday bash. Suzy was nowhere to be seen, not that TJ was surprised. She doubted Suzy had spent much time in the flat since meeting her dreamboat attacker. She poured herself a large cup of tea and slumped down onto the sofa, remote in hand, and prepared to watch some totally dreary chick flick. It seemed like a lifetime ago that TJ and Suzy had sat watching girly films, laughing about how stupid the women were in them. But now, here she was, doing the exact same things.

Allowing the film to play out in the background, she began to thumb through the pages of the accommodation section of the paper. Her eyes widened as she came across the perfect place. Grabbing the phone, she called the number and after a short conversation, made an appointment to view it immediately. She grabbed her keys and ran out of the door, forgetting all about Adam.

The place was perfect; it was a little converted outbuilding. The owner had restored it to try to make a bit of money to cover the costs of running his printing business in the main building. It was plain brick outside, junk scattered around the yard.

"I will be clearing all that up of course." The owner scratched the back of his neck, she got the impression no one had expressed an interest in this place. That just made her love it more.

"The interior has been cleared out and a kitchen and bathroom installed but obviously it's kinda a doer-upper."

TJ held her heart in her mouth as the key turned in the lock and she caught her first glimpse of the building. It was small, the floor remained bare concrete, the girders still visible in the ceiling. Temporary walls had been placed to partition off a bedroom; her eyes were drawn to a door at the back.

"There is a little bit of land out there, but again it needs work. Sorry." The owner sighed heavily, believing this to be another time waster.

The door led to a small patch of land, totally overgrown. A patch of grass was surrounded by cowslips and nettles that jostled to be higher and wider than the other. Butterflies and bees moved between the wild flowers that fought for their space in the garden. TJ turned to the owner.

"It's perfect, how soon can I move in?"

"Eh? Are you sure?" The owner stepped back, totally shocked that such a lovely, young woman would want to live in such a wreck of a building. "The machinery gets a bit loud at points, printing machines and that. That be okay?"

"I can pay one month bond and one month upfront to secure it."

The man frowned at TJ as she rummaged around in her bag and retrieved an envelope of money. After a pause, he took the envelope and split the contents in half.

"Why don't you keep the bond and use it to do the place up?" he smiled warmly. "I don't think a bond is needed, I mean, it's not like you could leave this place in a worse state than it is now!" He chuckled and handed TJ the key.

For over an hour TJ just walked around, stroking walls and dusting off cobwebs. Never before had she owned her own place, no flatmate, no parents, this was all hers. Her camera whirled as she shot picture after picture of every inch of the place, inside and out. The sun began to set and the butterflies and bees were replaced with moths, and her delight was complete when TJ saw several bats fly out of the printing workshop and begin to feast.

Bugsy was going to love it here.

Adam pulled into the car park just as Malika returned from a dog walk. She stared at him sternly.

"And just where is that fine lady of yours today?" She stood before him with her hand on her hip waiting for his reply.

"She's at her house, I would imagine," he replied nonchalantly.

"That's not where she was this morning." Malika pursed her lips together, trying to avoid a smile.

"Oh, for fuck's sake! Are there no women in my life that can keep their mouths shut?" he spat out, enraged that everyone was talking behind his back.

Malika may have been little but she still managed to swipe Adam around the back of the head for his language.

"Bulldog's kennel needs re-fixing; he has eaten through the fence, again!" Malika instructed. "Oh and there are two sinks in the washroom that are blocked."

"Call a bloody plumber then, Malika!" Adam roared. "Christ, that's what the money is there for."

Once again Adam felt the back of Malika's hand.

"That's what you are here for, Adam. You might be a high and mighty businessman at the office, but here, here you are still that little snotty boy with a bad attitude and a temper, that needs hard work to keep him grounded."

The standoff lasted mere seconds before Adam caved and headed towards the washroom, grabbing a tool box as he passed. Malika smiled triumphantly, she loved the bones off that boy. They were very few men in the world with his compassion, loyalty and modesty. She had always thought of him as a son since the day he asked for work, he was so keen to help out, so happy when a dog was re-homed. She was extremely proud of him, but now he needed to start a new life of his own and she thought TJ would be the perfect woman to help him do that.

It had taken three hours to unblock all the dog hair from the sinks and mend Bulldog's fence. Not that the brute had helped; all the while Bulldog would pick up his tools and move them, or lick his face in an attempt to get him to play with him. He was now filthy and stunk of dogs, if he was going to make himself presentable for his mother he would have to leave now and get showered.

Stripping off his work suit, he noticed a sign hanging over one of the dogs' kennels.
"You are joking!" He barged into the office where Malika sat with Aslan perched on her shoulder. "Who the hell did you get to adopt that dog? He is on his last legs."

The dog he referred to was a beagle, at least that's what they guessed he was. He had overgrown teeth that jutted out over his lips giving him a bulldog look. His eyes were puffy and bulged out, his legs bowed and he was on medication for a heart condition. Adam could not believe that Malika would home him out to someone in this condition.

"Here's the thing..." she began, "...it would seem that someone, not mentioning any names, ADAM, gave out a voucher for lifelong care of any dog. Food, medicine, vets bills, the lot."

Adam slowly began to realise what had happened.

"So, this 'recipient' came to have a meeting and instead of adopting a cute puppy or dog that lots of people wanted..."

"She took the one that no one would want," Adam finished off for her.

"She said that all the others had a good chance, whereas this one was never going to get another home. She figured that as she had been given the voucher as a gift, she should use it to give a gift to a dog."

Adam closed his eyes, of course TJ adopted this one, he cost the centre a fortune in vet's bills, and no one would look at him twice. No one except TJ. Adam shook his head, she never ceased to surprise him, always kind but at the same time she was strong and a formidable force. Malika slid a piece of paper out of a brown cardboard file.

"She just called, apparently she has found the perfect home for them both, I guess one of us should go check it out." She waved the piece of paper with the new address on in front of his face. "And don't forget to take Bugsy; he will need to have an investigation around the place to see if he likes it."

Adam cringed as the smell of this dog filled his car; strings of saliva hung from its mouth, its face in a permanent gurn. "You are one ugly dog." The dog turned to stare at him with its bulging eyes and tilted head.

The Sat Nav advised him to turn into what appeared to be an old factory. Yes, this had TJ written all over it, no high class apartment for her. Leaving Bugsy in the car he strode over to the house, of course the door was wide open! The place was tiny, everything merged into one room, and hearing TJ's voice he moved to the back door.

She was bathed in dusk's light, up to her waist in nettles; she was beautiful, natural, as though she belonged in the wild. It was a strange feeling that began to flow over him, like warm honey. The more he watched her the more relaxed he felt. It was like coming home.

"Shit, Adam, you scared the living crap out of me!" TJ complained. She waded through the undergrowth, clambering until she finally reached him. They stood before each other as though in battle, neither one wanting to be the first to move. Adam cracked first and lifting his head he pressed his lips against hers. Even the briefest of kisses stirred him up, tingling pins and needles shot through his body. TJ pressed herself closer to him and the gentle welcome kiss soon began to get out of control. He pushed her back slightly.

"Nice place," he smiled, staring into her beautiful eyes. Those eyes that saw the world so differently to everyone else. He could lose himself in her eyes, so bright, her pupils dilated in obvious response to him. "I like it," she smiled back. Slowly she began to back him into the house.

"Wait. I have a moving in present for you." He released himself from her reluctantly and went to retrieve the ugly mutt from the car, hoping it hadn't caused too much damage.

The dog strutted into the room like he owned the place. TJ squealed with delight and all thoughts of christening her new home evaporated like the angel's share of a whiskey barrel.

"I cannot believe he's here!"

"I cannot believe you chose that flea-bitten runt."

"Sshh." TJ covered the dog's ears. "You can't say that."

The dog observed her with its bug eyes watering and then, obviously satisfied, licked a slimy tongue over her arm.

"He won't win any beauty contests, that's for sure. I guess I had better get him back." He moved forward to lead the dog back to the car. TJ blocked him.

"What do you mean 'get him back'?" Adam took a step back, suddenly becoming aware that he had obviously done the wrong thing. "If you think he is coming here, seeing his new home, then going back, then you're an idiot. He is home now and he is not going anywhere!" Her once beautiful eyes now narrowed in a warning glare.

"But it's my mum's birthday," he began to protest. "This is just a visit. You could pick him up after."

TJ now struggled, she had a gift for his mum but there was no way she was leaving Bugsy, or taking him back to the kennels. A solution sprung to mind.

"I will get a sitter," she announced, standing to grab her phone off the side.

"You are gonna cause me some serious problems, mate," Adam muttered to the dog. Bugsy just blinked at him, circled around several times on TJ's jacket and slumped down with a huge sigh.

Chapter 16

"THANKS, MUM," TJ CROONED as her mother took Bugsy's leash.

"Erm, that's what we are here for, sweetie." She nervously smiled and turned to Adam. "What the hell sort of dog is it?" she asked out of TJ's earshot. Adam just laughed and shrugged his shoulders.

"I will pick him up tonight," TJ promised.

"You will not," her father's voice came from the tattered, old shed. "Go and have a good time, collect him in the morning, we can take care of..." Words failed him as he left the shed and came face to face with Bugsy. "Wow. Looks a little like Marty Feldman."

Showered and dressed, Adam now sat behind the wheel of his car; a faint smell of dog remained, wafting through the air. TJ was again muttering beside him.

"TJ, if you ask me one more time I am going to throw you out of the window!"

TJ had been fretting over Bugsy since she left him at her parents' house. She had suddenly become a first time mum leaving her child for the first time.

"Maybe I should ring and check?" she pondered, pulling her mobile out of her bag. Adam flicked on the indicator and pulled over to the side of the road. Before TJ had time to question him, he took the mobile out of her hand and put it into her bag. The sternness in his eyes immediately calmed her and a sly, guilty smile emerged. "Sorry," she muttered and gave him a quick peck on the lips. Adam's stomach turned, he wanted more. TJ backed away. "Get it under control, man! We're off to your parents." She giggled as his intense eyes devoured her.

"To be continued, Tabby Cat."

Once again the house took TJ's breath away, so beautiful and stylish. Every flower you could think of blended perfectly, a symphony of colour to greet you. Adam watched her as she slowly walked to the door, drinking in every drop.

"Thought I heard your tank pull up." Robert stepped out from behind the door. "When was the last time you got that thing serviced?" he joked.

"Piss off, my car runs like a dream," Adam barked.

"Mmmm, must be the way you drive it then."

Adam shot him the finger whilst simultaneously pulling him into a manly hug.

"So, this is the famous TJ?" Robert released Adam and headed towards her. "If you fancy upgrading...?" TJ chuckled as Adam rolled his eyes and introduced his best friend.

TJ was unaware that Robert already knew all about her. He had been the person Adam had turned to after the gallery disgrace. The one person he felt close enough to, to seek advice from, Robert knew everything about Adam and vice versa.

Adam had been at school just three days before he got into his first fight. At twelve years old he started high school and could not stay out of trouble the whole time he was there. His temper would rise quickly, and a few harsh words often turned into a full on fight. His parents had tried desperately to help their son. They knew his brother's death had a major impact on his life, as it did with all of them. But Adam was just a ball of anger all the time, it was not healthy.

He spent most of his days in detention with Mr. Rawlings, which was where he had met Robert. It was a strange pairing; Robert was always quiet, calm and did not seem to be a troublesome lad. It was his actions that landed him in trouble, whilst Adam lashed out at anyone who had a go at him; Robert took his time, waited and then took his revenge. He had never raised a fist to anyone, he would linger in the shadows, causing trouble until eventually someone else would do his dirty work for him. They had spent the whole of high school glued together, looking after each other.

Adam had pushed Robert to go on to university, he was smart and would breeze through, while he knew school was not right for him and decided he could make a go of it on his own. By the time Robert graduated, Adam had a business ready to go and now had a smart graduate to help run it.

"Jem!" Adam's mother cried out as all three came through the house and out into the garden. "I am so pleased you came." She pulled TJ into a firm embrace. "I was just talking about you to some friends about your work, you simply must meet them."

"Mother, no pimping TJ out today! This is your day, relax." Adam reclaimed TJ and wrapped a protective arm around her. His mother sighed loudly at this act, smiling between the two of them.

"Oh, stop this sickly, gooey show of emotion, I am gonna throw up!" Robert pretended to gag and Barbara smacked him firmly on the arm.

"Maybe if you found yourself a nice girl, Robert, then you would enjoy seeing your best friend happy!"

"Yeah or a nice guy!" Adam chimed in.

"Oh you're so funny." Adam and Robert began a play fight and TJ decided this would probably be a good time to give Barbara her gift.

"I hope you like it." TJ held her breath as Barbara tore open the brown package, her hand shot to cover her mouth as she saw the contents. Tears swelled and overflowed as Barbara saw the. Derek moved over to comfort his wife. Upon seeing the gift he too began to shed a tear. TJ's heart sank; oh God, had she done the wrong thing? Had she upset them when she only wanted to make them happy? She turned to Adam as though to seek his advice. She received little comfort from his expression. He stood staring, emotionless then, without warning stormed off. TJ was speechless, what could she say?

"You angel." Barbara's gentle words brought her back from her bemusement. Barbara reached out and held TJ's hand. "How did you...?"
"When I was last here, you said you wished you had a family portrait."

TJ had gathered photographs of all the family, then of Brian. She had skilfully crafted them all together to form a family portrait, then transferred it onto canvas, producing a large picture.
Everyone began to gather around them saying wonderful, kind things and Barbara wiped away her tears, replacing them with a glowing smile.
"I've got this," Robert's voice whispered in her ear. "You go sort his lordship out."

Adam sat on the garden swing, rocking to and fro. He was angry. Scrap that, he was furious with her. Why did she keep doing this? How could he be so angry at her but at the same time love her for what she had done? "Holy shit!" His eyes closed, was that what it was? Did he love her? He had said it in jest before but now, just now he had realised it. He was completely in love with her. He raised his eyes as he heard footsteps coming towards him, his blood began to boil again the minute he saw her.

"I just wanted to ..."

He shot a thunderous glare at her, his face almost grey.

"Wanted to what, TJ? Make everything better? Make it all go away? Did you think you could put up a picture of Brian and we could all pretend to play happy families?" His voice had raised, he knew he was shouting at her but he couldn't help it. She had taken a picture of his brother, taken a part of Adam and his family. "Why did you do it?" he spat as he spoke.

TJ recoiled slightly. "Your mother," she replied quietly. "She told me the one thing she wished for was that she had taken a picture of all of you when Brian was alive. The family together, it made her sad that she didn't have that. She has been so good to me, Adam; I just wanted to give her the one thing she wished for. That is what I am good at, photographs, putting emotions into a single frame."

Adam stood up. "Not all of us want to feel those emotions." He almost growled at her, "I think you should go."

"Adam, I..." TJ did not get her words out, Adam had turned his back on her and was now walking slowly back to the house.

"Thanks for the lift, Robert." TJ sat in the car as Robert drove her home, the house becoming a speck in the distance. Robert had come hunting for TJ and found her exactly where Adam had left her. She had asked him to call her a taxi but Robert was having none of that.

"You mustn't blame yourself, TJ; he struggles with anything to do with Brian." He smiled sympathetically. "You have to remember who you did this for, it wasn't for that dickhead, it was for Barbara, and let me tell you I have never seen her so happy. What you did was amazing."

TJ remembered how tightly Barbara had held her hand, how the tears had glistened against her cheek. He was right, this was for Barbara, it made her happy, but it didn't help that she had pissed Adam off by doing so.

"Why don't we head for a drink?" Robert suggested. "I only live round the corner." TJ eyed him warily; was Adam's best friend hitting on her? He saw the concern in her face and reassured her it was just a drink. "I promise you, nothing untoward, just a bit of a bitching session about the dickhead."

How could she refuse that?

Chapter 17

ROBERT'S APARTMENT WAS JUST as nice as Adam's; it felt a little more homely. She saw all the photos on his wall, most of them featured Adam or his family.

"Coffee? Tea? Beer? What's your poison?" Robert stood behind her, "I know, it's like a shrine, isn't it. Anyone would think I loved the man!" He snorted.

"You've known each other a long time then?" TJ asked, "...and beer is fine."

Robert grabbed two beers from the fridge and slumped down onto the sofa. "Most of my life." He raised the beer bottle to his mouth, taking a large swig.

"You have family of your own?"

"Oh wow, you are like a little reporter aren't you, straight in for the interrogation!" He smiled as he spoke.

"Just because I ask, doesn't mean you have to answer."

She studied his face as he watched her. He was really quite handsome, not Adam handsome, but he was striking. His eyes glistened naughtily as though always hiding a secret.

"My father passed away but he never really featured in my life. My mother, however, was amazing, she worked and raised me, I never went without a thing. I was a bit of a horror when I was younger, always getting into trouble. I think I was a bit of an attention seeker. Anyway, Adam and I became friends and I became really close to his family. Especially when my mother died."

He took another swig of his beer to drown the memories. His mother had always been so strong and beautiful; he admired her in every way. In an attempt to earn extra money to pay off his student loans, she had been involved in a scam which had landed her in prison. From that day he had watched her disappear, every visit she appeared thinner and more vacant. It destroyed him seeing his mum like that. She was usually so glamorous, particular about her appearance. When he studied some of the great poets, he had always pictured her as the heroine. But in there she was a mess; her hair pulled tightly back, no makeup, no fancy clothes. The last visit she had hardly spoken to him, he had tried to hold her hand in a comforting gesture but she had just pulled away. The next day they had found her hanging in her cell.

"Wow, I am just excelling myself today at putting my great big foot in my mouth!" TJ tried to lighten the mood. Robert replaced his painful expression with his usual cheeky one.

"So what the hell attracted you to Adam? I mean despite his good looks, his ever-growing bank account, and his wonderfully kind heart. Or was it the night on the balcony that sold him to you?"

TJ nearly spat out her drink "He told you about that?" She was mortified, burying her head in her hands, she dreaded to think about Adam's version of events. Robert obviously found it most amusing and laughed so hard he spilt his beer.

"Oh, come on, like you didn't tell your girlfriend about it!"

TJ knew this was true, but it was her humiliation to share. She sat quietly fuming as she drank the remains of her bottle.

"He told me about the gallery too." Roberts face was more serious now. "He was really worried, angry at himself. He was scared he had pushed you away, that's when I knew."

TJ cocked her head to one side in confusion. Robert continued, "I knew he had fallen for you. It takes a lot for Adam to lose his temper these days. We used to have competition to see who could light his fuse when he was younger, but now, now it rarely happens. The night of the gallery, he nearly put my table through. Moody git."

Her anger began to fade. "I don't know why he was worried? I mean, it was consensual."

"That's the point, TJ. He saw red, couldn't clearly remember what the hell had happened or who agreed to what. I was so pleased when you turned up at his office; he needs a good woman in his life. Someone who can embrace the monster inside him." The love and concern oozed from him and TJ started to become embarrassed, a change of topic was needed.

"So how come you have no lady in your life, Robert? You are clearly good looking, funny, well off and seem a really nice guy. What is wrong with you?"

Robert let out a loud raucous laugh. "It would take me all day to tell you what is wrong with me and mostly it's that word you used. 'NICE'. Don't you women know that being called 'nice' is the ultimate kick in the teeth?"

The conversation came to a halt when there was a knock at the door. "I will give you three guesses as to who that is." Robert opened the door to a dishevelled Adam. He then opened the door wide. Adam came face to face with TJ, sitting on Robert's sofa.

"What the fuck is going on?" he snarled at Robert, who immediately threw up his hands in surrender.

"Shut up and get in here, grab another beer on your way in," TJ snapped as she waved her empty bottle.

Adam skirted around Robert, his eyes never leaving him. To Robert's amusement he even backed into the room a little, refusing to turn as though something was going to happen the minute he turned his back.

"Told you," Robert said to TJ. "A total dickhead."

It took several hours, and several beers, before Adam finally calmed himself. Barbara had torn him to pieces after she learned he had made TJ leave. She had been livid with him and had not held back in telling him so, right in front of all their friends. TJ explained that she understood he was angry but also that she had done it for Barbara, not him. Robert had tried to back her up but Adam had shot him down quickly, so it was decided that they would change the subject and agree to disagree. The evening lightened after that and TJ had listened to all their stories, Adam and Robert at school, at home, when they first started to work together. She did not think that she had laughed so much, her sides ached and she had to hold her jaw to stop from laughing again as Robert retold a story of Adam and an old girlfriend.

It was close to one in the morning before they decided to call it a night; all had drunk far too much to consider driving, so Robert had made up his spare room for them.

TJ helped herself to the last piece of pizza they had ordered.

"Hey, greedy, don't you know it's not polite to not share!" Robert smacked her hand away and made a grab for the piece himself.

"Hey, I'm a guest." The two began a tug of war until the piece ripped in two. Laughing, they scoffed it down before Adam returned from the bathroom. Robert leaned in and kissed TJ on the top of her head. "Goodnight, sweet lady."

"Thanks for letting me stay, Robert, and thanks for bringing me here."

"Oh yeah, thank the guy who was trying to get off with his best friend's girl!" Adam called out as he returned. Simultaneously, Robert and TJ both threw cushions at his head. He dived behind the chair to duck them.

"So is that what I am now?" TJ asked, "...your girl."

Adam just smiled, "I think you are a lot more than that."

"There you go with that 'think' again. You know for a top businessman you seem to have a lot of trouble making decisions, Mr. Morgan," she said playfully.

"Maybe you should tell Adam how you feel first," Robert shouted out from his room.

TJ and Adam broke into laughter again, holding their sides in pain.

TJ cleansed her face with the cool water, the beer now churning in her stomach, her head beginning to spin. The paleness of Adam's face as she entered the room told her he was feeling the same. He handed her a t-shirt that Robert had laid out for her. She screwed up her face, refusing it and stripped off naked, climbing into the cool sheets. Adam admired her body, those sleek curves, her beautiful breasts.

Damn him for drinking so much. Sighing loudly, he too relieved himself of his clothes and slid in next to her. How he was going to make it through the night without leaping on her, he had no idea.

The single bed allowed no space and so their two bodies were pressed up against one another.

"I am sorry," TJ murmured, almost asleep already.

"Me too," he admitted as he reached over to her and wrapped his arm around her. She turned and snuggled into his chest. Her slender body caressed his side, her breasts flattened against him, her leg leisurely thrown over his. It should have been a very erotic gesture, their bodies entwined, but somehow it wasn't. It was more. He felt relaxed and at peace, the stress of the day leaving him in waves as he felt her gentle breathing against his chest. He wanted to stay like this forever, both protecting each other. Loving each other. Could this be? Could he finally have found the woman for him? She was so different, so unpredictable; he wondered if he could ever live like that. His life was so organised and clean cut, he was not sure if he liked the person she provoked out of him.

TJ stirred and her knee raised up to gently nudge his balls, as he muttered an expletive under his breath. He could feel her against his thigh, her soft curls tickling him. He wasn't that drunk, wasn't so drunk he didn't react to her body. But she was softly snoring now, just a low purr coming from his Tabby Cat's lips. He tried to gently push her knee away from him but that just resulted in a long, sexy sigh as she manoeuvred herself again.

Shit, this night was going to last forever.

She was going to pay for it in the morning.

Chapter 18

TJ FELT A TWANG OF GUILT as she stepped out of
the taxi. Adam had been curled around her so tightly
when she woke; it had been a wonderful feeling. But
she was so desperate to get back to her new baby.
Bugsy had stayed at her parents' and she wanted so
much to check on him and let him know that she was
still there for him and would be taking him home.

"Morning, darling," TJ's mother sang out as she saw
her heading up the path. TJ cringed as the volume
rattled her brain, stinging the delicate hangover she
was trying to avoid. Her mother gave her a knowing
nod and went to immediately put the kettle on.

Following her father's voice, she moved round to the
back of the house to find her father chatting to
Bugsy. She smiled at the pair of them, her father
seated in one chair with a coffee in hand, Bugsy
settled in the chair next to him like a pair of old men.
His ears pricked up as he heard TJ's footsteps.

"Hey, baby," she crooned as the dog tilted its head to one side, allowing her to scratch his ear but refusing to leave the comfort of his chair. She couldn't wait to get him home again, to move all her stuff and start making a home for herself. An empty space beckoned for her to leave her mark.

"Morning, mate." Robert sat at the table, a newspaper spread before him. "There is fresh coffee on." He nudged his head towards the machine without lifting his eyes from the paper.
"You seen TJ?" Adam asked grumpily, already guessing she had gone. All hopes of easing the tension in his groin eliminated.
"You look like a man that didn't get any last night," Robert teased.
"Fuck off!"

Two cups of coffee later began to see Adam's mood lift. Slightly. Robert had given his approval over TJ, and told him he would be insane if he didn't snap her up immediately. Adam knew this, but how TJ could ever fit into his life was beyond him. Robert was heading off to work and so Adam grabbed his keys and headed home to get a shower and changed. Maybe he would head into work just to check on everything. If TJ could leave without so much as a goodbye, then why should he go running after her?

The tension was odd as he walked into the café; usually it was full of conversations, laughter. It was the one place Adam loved to come to, he felt a jolt of life as he entered.

Today, however, this was not the case.

Robert greeted him, "Thank God you're here, I was just about to call you." The concern on Robert's face had him worried; Robert did not get flustered over anything. Before he had a chance to ask, two men came from the office, one in police uniform, one plain clothes.

"I am the owner, Adam Morgan." He held out his hand to both men. "Is there something wrong?"

The uniformed officer spoke first. "We are investigating a suspicious death, we just need to ask you a few questions." He held out a photograph of a young woman, very beautiful. "Can you tell me if you recognise this woman?"

Adam shook his head and passed the photograph to Robert, who immediately covered his mouth with his hand.

"Yes," he nodded solemnly. "She used to come in here regularly, with work colleagues mostly. I think she worked for some agency or publishers, something like that. Oh God, it's not her, is it?"

The officer retrieved his photograph. "This is Camilla, she was found last night, her body was found under a bridge. It would appear that she has been there a while, if you know what I mean."

The older man nudged the younger cop in the ribs at this callous comment. "I apologise," he continued.

"We have been advised that there was an incident here involving her, about a year ago, do you have any recollection of this?"

"Yes." Again Robert answered for Adam. "Do you remember, Adam? I had to call you, some guy was hassling her, he grabbed her I think, anyway, another customer punched him and she ran out. The police came round about an hour or so afterwards and we gave statements."

Adam now recalled the event. "Yes, that's right. Wasn't it that guy that always used to hang around at the bar, always on his own? You talked to him a bit, didn't you, Rob?"

"Tray? Trevor? I think it was something like that?" Robert tried to remember.

"Did he ever pay with a credit card? Or mention where he lived? Anything useful?" The uniformed officer was writing everything down in his little notebook. How they managed to fit all their information in those things baffled Adam. They must go through one of those things every hour!

"I can't believe it." Adam gripped Robert's shoulder as he spoke. "She spent all that time, alone, under a bridge. Why the hell did no one find her earlier?" Adam shook his head; the thought of it filled him with fear. It must have been cold, damp and dark under there; she just lay in the undergrowth, slowly decomposing. He shuddered, suddenly thinking of her poor family, her poor parents.

Adam saw Robert's pale face. "Come on, let's have a drink." Robert slowly followed him into his office. One of the staff brought in two cups of steaming hot tea.

"Do you think he did it?" Roberts asked in disbelief, "I mean, I spoke to him, laughed with him. I saw him come in that day. Christ, you don't think it was that day, do you?" A grey shadow fell over his face, his eyes wide.

"Robert, whatever has happened is nothing to do with us or you. Has he been in here since?" Adam asked, suddenly realising that he could have a murderer in his precious sanctuary.

How could this happen? This poor young girl, why hadn't anyone noticed her missing? Come to see them before now?

"I'd better talk to the staff, ask around." Robert switched into manager mode. "Maybe some of the night staff have seen him, or spoken to him. Anything might help, right?"

"Of course, mate. You do the staff and I will put a mail out to all the other cafés to see if anyone else recognises him."

The two friends set to work trying to help as much as they could. All staff were contacted, whether they were on a day off or not. Photos were distributed around the business, all over the UK. A few people had recognised him; they had given an impression of a sad, angry man. A few of the female staff had been forced to call security over when he had tried to hit on them. Adam and Robert gathered every little piece, every description, every comment, anything that people remembered. After several exhausting hours Adam called up the officer who had left his card and passed all the details over to him, emails, faxes, everything they had.

They felt a little lighter afterwards, hoping that somehow they could help bring this bastard to justice.

"It's long overdue," Robert had scowled.

Chapter 19

"WELL? WHAT DO YOU THINK?"

Frank Benton threw the files onto his desk. Why the hell did he have to get mixed up in this? He should have retired from the police force years ago, but no, here he was sitting with a multiple murder case facing him.

He skimmed through all the notebooks, taking in everything the guys at the café had told him. They seemed nice enough blokes, genuinely upset that this had happened to one of their customers.

There lay the problem.

It wasn't just one.

Losing interest in waiting for an answer to his question, the younger officer took himself off to get a coffee, leaving Frank staring blankly at all the papers.

The lad was a good cop, Frank felt that he brought a lot of insight to his investigations, new ideas and techniques Frank had never heard of. Sometimes though, he just needed quiet so that he could think without the boy's constant analysis. But he was young, cocky and arrogant. A bug he would have to bear.

Flicking through the file, he held up a photograph of the young girl, Cam. She was so young, so beautiful, nothing he hadn't seen before. But there was something about the way the body had been positioned. She had been found with her hands over her heart, a flower placed between her fingers. It was creepy. Frank was immediately reminded of another case, another girl found just two months before. Her file remained on his desk at the bottom of a huge pile. No family had reported her missing; no friends were trying to find her. No one had any idea who she was - just another runaway that came to a bitter end.

Frank studied the board that displayed all the evidence that had been gathered so far, it was not much. Ribbons of blood red linked one picture to another, one article in a newspaper to another, a spider web of information that told him precisely nothing. But his gut told him they were connected, not that he had mentioned this to anyone. No one wanted to admit a serial killer was on the loose. But the two girls, both found in similar positions, no sexual assault, no damage to the bodies, except the thin red line around their necks.

The discovery of the second woman had opened a few more avenues to explore. She had immediately turned up on the missing persons reports. Frank had been able to speak to her family, friends and her boss, who had been extremely helpful. She had given Frank a detailed report of the woman's life. It would seem she was quiet, didn't go out that much, certainly not a party girl. There were, however, two interesting pieces of information. One - friends had said she was dating someone online, no one had met him yet and so knew little about him. Two - there had been an assault in a café, it had been reported but no follow-up made. This is what had led him to The Coffee Café. The owner and manager had agreed to talk to all staff and gain as much information as possible. They may uncover some information, they may not. If he knew something from all his years in service, it was that nothing was certain. This may just end up another dead end case in a dusty old file room.

Sometimes the bad guys got away.

"Frank, phone call on line three."
What joys would this phone call bring, Frank wondered? As he pressed the button on his phone, his mood immediately lifted.
"Sara, how lovely to hear from you. How are you?

He cradled the phone to his ear, Sara was an old friend. She had got herself into a heap of trouble a few years back, her boyfriend had tried to set her up but Frank had helped straighten it all out. One of the rare success stories.

"I'm fine, Frank, just thought I would check in with you," Sara cooed fondly.
"How's the weather in New York?" he asked.

They chatted for a while, catching up on all that had happened, Sara was staying with her partner and some friends over there. It sounded beautiful. Frank regretted not travelling when he was younger. His sister, Mary, had always had big ideas and dreams but as with most people, life got in the way.

"Tell me, Sara; is your better half with you?" Frank suddenly had an idea. Jamie, Sara partner, was a bit of a computer whizz. Without giving out details, he explained that he wanted an easy way to go through all the till receipts in all the chains, that he needed to find visa card receipts to try and get any sort of lead.
"Jesus, Frank, in a place like that there could be thousands of receipts. More. Without some idea of dates and times it would be a needle in a haystack. With just a 'possible' first name it would be impossible. I'm sorry."
"Just a long shot." Frank grinded his teeth together in frustration.
"Okay, Frank," Jamie began. "We are back next week, see what this café place digs up and I will come in

and see if we can't filter the system somehow. Anything is better than nothing, right? As you keep telling me 'there is always a paper trail'."

Frank thanked them both and agreed to meet up in a few days. He thought very highly of Sara and Jamie. It had been Jamie who had discovered most of the evidence that helped Sara, they had been together ever since.

Chimes rang out on his laptop as he gazed into thin air. Sometimes, he found clearing his mind helped to find new ideas. He clicked on the email icon to see a large file from the coffee shop. When opened, it contained statements from various staff members, mostly female, who had seen or served this guy. Each statement listed the date and rough time that they thought the guy had been there. The general opinion was that his name was Troy.

Frank sneered at the screen. Now he had a name, dates, and with a bit of luck security cameras would have picked up an image of him. Once he had a face, that was all he needed. A face would produce interest, people who knew him, landlords, dentists, neighbours. This would lead him to a full name, address, a workplace and hopefully if they could find some credit card details they would be able to track him and then catch the bastard before he hurt anyone else.

Grabbing a pen he strode over to the board and in big letters wrote, 'Suspect One – TROY'. Finally he was moving forward, and he circled the name three times before returning to his desk. Another officer walked past Frank's open door; seeing the large circles he took a step inside.

"Hey, you got a lead on the dead girl? Who's Troy?"

"Some dick," he muttered, not paying attention to the guy but staring intently at the name. "If God is smiling on me today, he will be a stupid dick who used his credit card to pay for his coffee."

Before the other officer had a chance to question him further he was pushed out of the way. Frank's heart sank; he did not need the lad to tell him what had happened. He had seen that expression time after time. He stood up and grabbed his coat.

"Where is it?" he asked walking past both men and heading towards the reception desk. The young lad had to trot to keep up.

"Down by Marshalls Glen, in a tunnel." He handed Frank a scrap of paper then slowed and returned to his desk.

"Hey, junior!" he called out to his younger colleague. "Get your shit together and get to the car. We got another body."

Chapter 20

AFTER EMAILING ALL THE INFORMATION to the police it was too late to do any work, so Adam decided to head home but a sudden need to see his parents had him diverting his route.

"Oh, come crawling in, have you?" Barbara scolded her son as he walked in. Adam had totally forgotten about the feud between them. It seemed like a lifetime ago. Barbara, however, had it fresh in her mind.

"Do not think that you can come here and..."

She never finished her lecture; Adam had crossed the room and smothered her in a tight embrace. He held her so tightly, feeling like a child again needing his mother's love. Barbara knew immediately something was wrong, so she did not push him but simply returned his embrace, waiting until he was ready to let her go.

"What's happened?" she asked as he finally released her. Derek moved over, clasping a firm hand on his son's shoulder.

"I'm sorry, Mum; I don't want to fight with you," his voice caught in his throat.

Slowly Adam began to retell the events of the day, his parents listening, his mother's hand never leaving his.

"Oh, that poor girl," Barbara sobbed. "We must do something, send something to her family."

"That would be lovely, I am sure we could sort something out," Adam replied, squeezing her hand in return. He couldn't imagine how they must feel, their daughter missing for so long and then found like that. Thoughts of her decomposed remains flooded his mind; he shook his head, trying to clear the horrific images.

"How's Robert? Did he know her?" Barbara's thoughts turned to the man she saw as her adopted son. "He must feel terrible. I will call him." Without needing anyone's approval she dashed off to the kitchen to retrieve her phone, immediately calling Robert.

"Are you okay, son? Really?" Derek stared at every inch of Adam's face, as though trying to read him.

"Yes, it's just a shock, that's all."

"Please don't think me cruel, son, but do you think this will affect business?"

Adam had not even thought about the publicity this would attract. His heart sank at the thought that people may not feel safe to come into the café. That's not what he wanted; he wanted a warm place that

welcomed everyone, that allowed everyone to be themselves.
He hated to do it, but he would have to contact people to help him with this. He felt terrible but his business had to come first.

The drive home felt longer than it ever had before. This was nothing to do with him, it wasn't his fault, it hadn't happened on his premises.

So why did he feel so damn guilty?

This young woman had left his café and never returned. Who knew what had happened to her? Had it happened straight after? His fist slammed into the steering wheel, frustration raging through him. Why? Why his place? He couldn't go home, the emotions flowing through him were clashing, like a storm in his brain, everything was becoming fuzzy.

One thing became clear.

He needed TJ.

He turned the car around and headed straight to her, every mile clearing his head as he thought of her. Her beautiful face, heart, body. She was waiting for him as he pulled up outside.

"Your mum called. She said you might come here." TJ opened her arms to him as he stepped out of the car. He ran to her, almost knocking her off her feet. He couldn't speak, didn't know what to say. He just knew he needed her now. Without mercy he found her lips, pushing his tongue in to meet hers. TJ clung to him, knowing what Adam needed.

She matched his need kiss for kiss. Their breath, hot and loud, fuelling the desire. Neither spoke as Adam kicked the door shut behind them. Grabbing her waist, he hoisted TJ up onto the small kitchen counter, grasping her legs to wrap around him. She needed no convincing, a small moan rumbling in her chest as she felt his need through his jeans.
"I need..."
TJ silenced him. "I know what you need, shut up and take me."

Adam was stunned by her words; he paused for a moment, taking a breath. TJ was already stripping her t-shirt off, bare-breasted underneath. Her eyes were wide, a wildness, almost anger flashed through them. Her breath was short and needy. As she raised a hand to cup her own breast, a rage took over Adam. How dare she? That was his job? How dare she touch them before him? He slapped her hand, a growl of disapproval evoking a sharp intake of breath from TJ.
"Mine," was the only word he could muster.

In seconds his trousers were gone and he was entering her, fast and hard. TJ screamed out as he pounded into her. All his worries leaving him. The stress and sadness flying from him.

Over and over again, he tried to rid himself of the angst, the wonderful bliss of losing himself in TJ. Her warm soft body tightly holding him in place. All too soon her body began to tense, she drew him in further and further until with a final scream she let go. Her nails dug into his back, her heels stabbing into him. He watched as she slowly began to relax, releasing her grip on him and sighing loudly. Her face was flushed, her lips still plump and red from his assault, perfection.

"You didn't?" TJ began but Adam swept her up.
"I haven't finished with you yet." He silenced her with a gentle, more loving kiss.

He realised his mistake pretty soon.
"You have no furniture in here!" he uttered, mortified that this was not going to continue in the bed. TJ just giggled.
"I have a blanket over there." She pointed over to the corner where a pretty ugly Bugsy was curled up.
"Shit!" His brain could not function as he desperately searched for somewhere to lay TJ down.
"Here." Scooting out of Adam's grip she gently moved the dog off the blanket and seductively swept it along the floor, Adam following. She opened the back door and laid the blanket on the small patch of grass. She had been busy, the garden was still wild but there was space in the middle to lie down. It was warm outside, the sun hanging on to light up the

smallest of parts of the skyline, a purple haze merging it with the night skies.

TJ reached up and pulled him to the ground next to her, rolling him onto his back she straddled him. Starting at the bottom she began one by one to slowly undo the buttons on his shirt. Each one revealing a sliver more of his toned, taut body. Her hands smoothed over his stomach as she moved higher. The wait was deliciously painful; she remained perfectly still, knowing the slightest move would ruin the moment. The final button popped and she opened his shirt wide. A small moan of approval caused her muscles to tense.

"Fuck," Adam hissed as his erection throbbed underneath her. He clutched at handfuls of grass as though trying to hold himself back. Leaning forward TJ placed her soft lips against his neck, now displaying a stubble, which added to the sexiness that was Adam Morgan.

She rained tiny kisses down his neck, over his chest and down over his stomach. She could feel his excitement pressing between her breasts. His breath rasped as the smallest movement she made caused lightning to shoot through his body. Every kiss, every touch burned his skin. Raising herself she lowered onto him, her breasts in full display in front of him, begging to be nipped and sucked. Her nipples erect and wanton. Once again he was inside her, deep inside. Her hips ground against him, taking every part of him in, comforting him with her soft embrace.

"I love you," he whispered, almost surprising himself as he said it out loud.

"I love you, too." She smiled and quickened her pace. Whether it was the pace or the words she had spoken, Adam did not know, but his body finally let go. Refusing to release her hips, Adam held her in place until every last wave had been ridden.

It was a few moments before both had caught their breath, not just from the amazing feelings but from the words they had finally admitted to each other. They lay on their backs, lost up amongst the stars that had begun to show. Millions of stars shinning down upon them both lying naked in the grass.

"It's a good job you have no neighbours," Adam chuckled, thinking about all the nosey people around his apartment and his mother's.

"I don't think there is a soul around here till about six-thirty in the morning."

"Just as well, the noise you make. Has anyone ever told you that you are very loud during sex?"

TJ smacked him firmly on the arm.

"Fuck off!" she shouted, her beautiful mouth forming an amazing smile.

"Thank you." Adam turned to her, "I just needed you, you make me feel like I can deal with anything."

"Adam, there's no need to thank me, and you can deal with anything. Look at what you have achieved, what you have lost. You are the most amazing man I have ever met, and stubborn," she joked. "So where do we go from here?"

Adam raised an eyebrow at her, puzzled.
"I mean, I have never really had anyone serious before. I mean dated anyone, people kinda flit in and out of my life."
"You have never dated?" he cried out, aghast. "Not even in school?"
"Nope, I was a bit of a dragon. I think I scared boys off, to be honest."

Adam hoisted himself up onto his elbows, "I'd like to take you on a date. If you want me to," he asked.
"I have just told you that I love you, so I guess I could." She shrugged her shoulders and giggled.

He loved her laugh, her whole face lit up but her eycs, her eyes glistened, reflecting the stars above.
"I love you, Tabby Cat."
"That name calling can stop then!" she complained. But also added, "I love you too, my first love."

Adam melted; his body felt like it had been slowly lowered into a warm bath.
He was her first love, she had never felt like this about anyone before, never had a relationship, just had a bit of fun. But Adam made her feel different, she felt happy and like she could be herself with him. She didn't have to pretend or control herself. He loved her for who she was.

"You are my first love too, TJ. I may have seen other women and had girlfriends before but no one like you. No one I truly loved."

He took her face into his hands and kissed her. Gentle and sweet, gathering the blanket as they both moved inside.

Chapter 21

THE HEADLINES THAT HIT the newspapers were exactly what Adam was dreading. They had repeatedly mentioned the café, painting it as some dark, dingy pick-up joint.

"Fuck!" Adam roared again as another paper went flying across the table. His business manager, Andrew, had given up trying to calm him down long ago. Instead he just stood to retrieve the paper.

"I want to sue, Andrew. I want these bastards eating their words." This time a coffee cup whizzed past Andrew's ear, barely missing him.

"Jesus, Adam!" He turned to see the coffee dripping down the wall, the cup in pieces beneath. "Feel better?"

"Don't start on me, Andrew," Adam warned.

"There is nothing to sue, they are writing a story. Yes, it doesn't read brilliantly for us, but bigger picture here, Adam. A woman was murdered, we have helped as much as we can and will continue to help. We have already organised fund raising for her family, no one is blaming us here."

"But here is where it fucking happened, isn't it!"

Andrew was getting nowhere fast. He almost cried out to a young intern who had entered the office to bring in more coffee.

"GET THE FUCK OUT! How dare you come in here without knocking! This is my office! You show respect!" Adam paced, unable to stop himself. The poor young boy's eyes widened and he sucked in his lip, trying not to cry. Andrew gave him a sympathetic smile and advised that he leave the coffee for now.

"And where the fuck do you think you're going?" Adam snarled as Andrew stood up.

Calmly he replied, "Don't take this out on me, Adam, or the staff. I know you are pissed but we don't deserve this. I am not staying in here to listen to your crap and abuse. I suggest you calm yourself down in whatever way is best and we will talk again. Better still, Adam, fuck off home!"

He slammed the door on his exit and Adam was left to stew on his own. He knew this was no one's fault, he knew the papers were just stating what happened. But this was his baby; this particular café had been the first one. He slumped into his leather chair, swinging it side to side. First. That's what TJ had declared to him, he was her first love.

The pain and anger began to subside, that calmness that she seemed to instil over him began to comfort

him, embracing him. The phone rang seconds before
he had a chance to reach for it himself. It was TJ.
"So I hear you have an unexpected day off."
Damn it, Andrew had phoned her the second he left
the building, how dare he control him like that?
TJ ignored his silence. "So, anyway, I need you to
come pick me and Bugsy up. We are off visiting."
"I am not having that mutt in my car, TJ; it will take a
week to get the stench out."
It was as though he hadn't spoken.
"Great, about half an hour then. Bye."
The line went dead.

What the hell had happened to him? He was a strong
businessman, had built it up from scratch and
controlled everything. So why all of a sudden was he
allowing everyone to tell him what to do? Why was
everyone taking it upon themselves to make
arrangements for him?
Sheepishly Anthony, Adam's assistant, popped his
head around the door waving a white flag.
Adam shook his head but allowed himself to see the
funny side.
Without speaking Anthony passed a brown paper
bag around the door and pushed it in with his foot as
though feeding a wild animal. Quick as a flash he left
the office again. Opening the bag Adam saw a
perfectly made up 'desk lunch', complete with
napkins and a cola. How did he do these things so
quickly? Adam made a note to himself to thank him
later, maybe a pay rise was in order. He did not want
to lose his 'man-Friday'.

"Are you intending to move some furniture in, at any point?" Adam quizzed as they entered the still barren place. This time, however, it was far from isolated. Cars were scattered outside, the building in front alive with sounds and noises as people worked and chatted. TJ just raised one eyebrow and huffed.
"You don't like my place? Don't come in my place!"
"I didn't," he answered grabbing her waist, "As I recall, I came outside!"

TJ slapped him on the arm playfully, but rose onto her tiptoes to kiss him. Before his thoughts could go any further, TJ pulled away and reached down to scoop Bugsy into her arms. The dog was as ugly as ever, strings of drool hanging from his mouth. The stench almost too much to bear.
"So, who are we visiting?"
"Ghost's new mum," TJ replied casually.

Ghost had been one of the dogs that TJ had met when he first took her to the shelter. It seemed that during the gallery evening, whilst Adam was busy complaining to Robert, TJ had spoken to many people about the dogs and found many of them homes. Ghost had been a particularly hard case; he had been starved, abandoned and left for dead. TJ had somehow found a unique bond with the animal and had returned several times to try and build a trusting relationship with him to allow him to find a new home.

It was only a short drive and TJ could not sit still waiting to see how Ghost was settling in. She had met the woman a number of times and they had discussed at length Ghost's behaviour. But today she felt Adam needed this more than her. The first time he took her to the shelter had been the most wonderful day. Seeing all these animals, having been treated so poorly but still longing for company, still fighting to stay happy had inspired her. She hoped it would do the same for Adam today, he needed it.

"TJ," a woman called out.
"Beth, how are you?" TJ kissed the woman's cheek affectionately. "Beth, this is Adam. Adam this is Beth."
"So, you took on our Ghost." Adam reached to shake the woman's hand; she knocked it away and leant in to kiss both cheeks.
"Goodness me, Adam, your photos do not do you justice. TJ, you need to seal the deal with this one. Quickly." She shot Adam a cheeky wink and showed them into the kitchen. He could see why TJ had warmed to her. Bugsy hauled himself out of the car and began to explore outside. "He's fine out here," Beth confirmed.

Ghost lay curled up in a little bed under one of the kitchen counters. It was strange seeing him lying down, as he was always leaning against the wall in his kennel.
"He had sores over his legs," Beth explained as she made a pot of tea. "Probably from lying on hard

concrete too much when he was abandoned. They will have been very painful. But we have had some treatment, it's ongoing but he is a lot more comfortable now." She placed the pot of tea, along with cups and milk, onto a tray and moved into the lounge.

TJ made herself comfy on one of the overly large sofas, curling her legs up to one side. She had loved this house the minute she heard about it. It was a little cottage style house, set back in a large garden. There were no noisy neighbours or traffic that might scare Ghost. Beth lived on her own so he would have lots of opportunities to build a relationship up and hopefully learn to trust again.

As they chatted TJ heard the sound of claws clicking on the tiles in the kitchen. Ghost had decided to join them. The room fell silent as all three tried not to look, for worry of scaring him.

After walking around the room, he turned four or five circles on the rug in front of the fire and flopped down again.
"Oh my gosh." TJ's eyes filled with tears. "He has followed us in here."
Beth smiled. "I think he has decided he quite likes to be around people." She was like a proud mum, watching, as her child takes its first steps.
"What you have done with him is outstanding," commended Adam, now calm and relaxed. "I cannot believe he is the same dog."

"It is taking time," Beth explained, "It is so hard to not reach out and pet him. He sometimes comes right up and leans against my leg and I want to just hold him. But I know he is not ready yet. He will let me know when he's ready."

"I am so pleased you found each other. You are just perfect for him, and I have no doubt that in the future, when I visit, he will be curled up on your lap."

TJ took a large sip of her tea, trying to control her emotions.

"Oh God," Beth cried out, "Just how long are you intending to keep visiting for?"

TJ stuck her tongue out.

Getting Bugsy back into the car proved harder than getting him out. He had managed to find every little bit of dirt and grime he could, and then eaten it or rolled in it.

"I am not touching that!" Adam held his hands up in disgust at the mess. "Get a blanket; spread it out so it doesn't touch my seats."

"Oh, get a grip, Adam!" TJ began to get cross with him. "It's a bit of mud, and HE is not an 'IT'."

With a final shove, Bugsy fell into the car and settled himself on the blanket. TJ stormed around to the other side and got in.

"Are you not talking to me now?" Adam asked as they left the house behind.

"You are an arse sometimes. He's a dog! What the hell are you gonna be like when Bulldog comes to live with you?"

Adam was baffled; he had never mentioned anything about Bulldog coming to live with him. In fact he was sure he had explained that it would not be possible. His quizzical expression sent heatwaves through TJ.

"What the hell?" she cried out. "You have no intention of taking that dog, do you?"

Adam failed to reply.

"HE will NEVER find a home, you know that, don't you? He pines for you all the time, and is so happy when you visit. But you! You are just gonna leave him there for the rest of his life!"

She did not understand how he could do this; she had watched Adam with Bulldog. Seen how happy he was with him. How was it possible that Adam could even think about leaving him?

"TJ, you don't understand. He's too big, too loud, too clumsy. I could never fit him into my life." Adam tried to explain but TJ was not suppressed.

"I am big. I am loud. Does that mean you will not be able to fit ME into your life?" She was shouting now, loudly. "In fact, stop the car."

"What?" Adam said in disbelief. But TJ already had her seatbelt undone.

"STOP THE FUCKING CAR, NOW!"

Unable to deal with this and drive, Adam pulled over and turned off the engine. Before he had a chance to utter a word, TJ was out of the car and dragging Bugsy from the back seat.

"TJ, come on, be fair. Get back in the car." Adam tried to reason with her but TJ was already walking away. "TJ, come on. At least let me give you a lift home. A woman's just been found murdered, it's not safe!"

"Don't worry, if I am killed, I'll make sure they don't link me up with your precious, fucking café."

Chapter 22

SHE DIDN'T WANT TO WALK AWAY; she didn't mean the things she said. Every footstep away from the car was making her come to her senses. Her shoulders slowly lowered, her hands unfurled and her breath released itself in huge clouds. Why was it making her so mad? She knew Adam had a full life and there was no way Bulldog could fit into his apartment. She wasn't even cross with him about this. So what the hell was she so angry about?

The car had still not moved behind her. She dare not look for fear of Adam following her; she just could not deal with him at the moment. She needed to clear her head.
She needed Suzy.

Adam's hands gripped the steering wheel so tightly, his eyes transfixed on TJ. Every short breath was causing a surging pain through his chest. He wanted to go after her, tell her he was sorry. But sorry for what? His life was not like hers. He could not simply do whatever suited him, whenever it suited him. He had responsibilities, a role to fulfil. But filling that role had stopped him having any sort of life outside of work. The only friend he had was Robert and most of their time was spent at work.

TJ's silhouette was now almost out of sight. She had not glanced back, not once. He knew because he dared not blink in case she did. His eyes were sore and dry.

"What the hell just happened?" he blurted out; slamming his hands on the wheel he had been holding so tightly. He loved this woman. She loved him; he knew that in his heart. So why was it so God damn hard to have a relationship with her? This should be the easiest thing in the world to do, instead it was constant heartache. He had too much in his life for this; he could not afford to dedicate so much time to one person. He had a business to run, people depended upon him. Thoughts swirled round and round his mind, making him dizzy. He was pulled in two different directions, a fear crushing him, restricting him.

He didn't need this.

"TJ, you are crazy," Suzy squealed as they opened another bottle of wine. "Why are you pushing him away?
"Is that what I am doing? Oh what is wrong with me?"

Suzy chuckled, "You think you are this free spirit, that you are not bound by the constraints that the rest of us are bound by. But you know what? You're not!"

TJ screwed up her eyes, desperately trying to focus on Suzy's face that was rapidly smudging out of focus. Her vision seemed like she was using a soft focus lens on her camera, everything just a little warmer, colours blending together rather than fighting it out for attention.

"You see," Suzy continued, "You are just as controlling as everyone else. If something doesn't go your way you throw a hissy fit. You reject it. Adam doesn't comply with your set of rules so you are rejecting him!" She took another healthy swig of her wine.

"Just like Adam is rejecting Bulldog," TJ uttered in almost a whisper, sitting back on the blanket that was laid out in her little garden. Bugsy had his head hooked over her foot, his big eyes barely able to keep open. The long walk home had tired him out. She reached out and scratched his ear.

"You do know that is one ugly dog, don't you?" The sound of their laughter burst out over the noisy machinery that surrounded them.

"Enough about me. How is your love life with the attacker?"
Suzy slapped her on the arm, "Don't call him that! But yeah..." Suzy lay back on to blanket, allowing her

eyes to close to protect them from the glaring sun. "..He's, you know."

The corners of her mouth crept upwards and her mind seemed to drift off as she entered into a wonderful world of memories. TJ knew exactly what Suzy meant. She knew because that was exactly how she felt when she thought of Adam. The lovely warm thoughts soothed her mind as she closed her eyes.

The sudden silence woke TJ from the alcohol-induced coma she and Suzy had apparently slipped into. The factory was closing, all the machines now silenced, the chattering reduced to a few conversations as the workers returned to their cars. The blinding sunlight had been reduced to a golden glow as it began to disappear behind the building. A shadow beginning to creep over her legs, Bugsy was now tipped onto his back, snoring. His legs stretched out over his head, he looked so comfortable. Suzy began to stir, sensing TJ watching her.

"Holy fuck! What time is it? Shit, I should be at work." She staggered to her feet, still blinking hard, trying to focus. "Crap, crap, crap, crap." Grabbing her phone, she called a taxi to collect her from the main road. "Sorry, TJ, love you," she called out as she grabbed her bag and ran for the door.

"Just me and you then, handsome." Bugsy stirred but did not open his eyes. TJ knew what she needed to do, just not quite how to do it. She had to call him, had to apologise. She had known it the minute she got out of the car, but in typical TJ style, had gone too far to go back.

Reluctantly she dialled Adam's number.

No reply.

Unwilling to give up, she tried Robert's number.

"Sorry, TJ, I haven't seen him." He suggested a few places where he might be. TJ began to panic, what if she couldn't get in touch with him? Before she had a chance to try another number, the phone vibrated in her hand. It was Barbara.

"Hi, Jem, sweetie." She sounded cheerful, at least someone was today. "I wondered if you had a little spare time to pop round this evening, I will make dinner."

There was a long pause on the phone, neither one speaking before Barbara added, "I have asked Adam to join us. I think a good talk is in order, don't you?"

Had he talked to his parents? Of course he had, she had told her parents how she felt, it was only natural that Adam had also spoken to his.

"Yeah, that would be lovely," TJ replied; if she had to do this in front of everyone then so be it.

The taxi cab smelled of stale cigarettes, TJ found herself trying not to inhale through her nose to avoid the stench. The driver had talked nonstop since she got in, telling her about the weather, his kids, people he had driven so far today. It was relentless. TJ just wanted to sit back and rid herself of the hangover she was beginning to suffer from. This guy was just not helping. At least he wasn't expecting any response from her, he just warbled on and on and on.

The streets always felt different at night; the paths sparkled, reflecting orange sparks of light from the street lamps. Why did so many people fear the night? To TJ it was the most beautiful time, the darkness seemed to wrap everything up snug and tight. The stars above offered a spectacular view, their light almost as warm as the sun.

"Blimey, nice place," the taxi driver claimed as he pulled into the driveway. He wasn't wrong. It was a beautiful place; TJ remembered walking in for the first time. The evening of the charity ball when she had first seen Adam in his family home. Her heart began to thump hard, the thought of Adam stirring all sorts of questions. Was he angry? Was he cross that she had walked out on him? What if he didn't want anything more to do with her?

"Not being funny, love, but if you don't get out soon I am gonna have to charge you another mile's fare."
"Sorry." TJ handed over the money and stepped out onto the gravelled driveway. Each footstep crunched as she walked to the door. Barbara was waiting for her.
"Hello, my dear. Good grief, you look shocking."

Always straight to the point. "Thanks," TJ replied, immediately feeling at ease.

Barbara led her straight through to the garden.

"Is he here?" TJ asked, trying to sound calm.

Barbara just smiled at her. "You are a lovely girl, you know that, don't you?"

TJ lowered her head, slightly embarrassed.

"I knew the minute I met you, the minute I saw your work that you and Adam might get on. I hoped that you would. My son is a very rigid character. It takes a great deal to get him to admit his feeling. He is like a baby bird. With you, he is beginning to experience all sorts of emotions that I don't think he knew he had. He is struggling to make sense of it all." She stopped and turned TJ towards her. "Give him a chance, dear; don't let him push you away. We will get there with him. You and me together." She wrapped her arms around TJ and pulled her so close she could feel her thumping heartbeat. Her anxiety squeezing her chest, her throat dry, she now felt like crying. Why had she behaved so badly to him?

"Come on." Barbara stepped back. She straightened TJ's shirt collar and pushed a strand of loose hair from her eyes. "He is waiting for you."

Chapter 23

ADAM STOOD AT THE BOTTOM of the garden, his white shirt casually hanging over his blue jeans. She had never seen him so casual. If it was possible her heart began to beat faster at the sight of him. He was not just handsome, he was beautiful. She felt like she was floating towards him, this vision becoming closer and closer. He was bathed in a soft glow of fairy lights that had been strewn through the branches of the trees. He reached out to her and she captured his hand, causing sparks to fly, freezing her to the spot, unable to take her eyes off the entwined hands.

"I still want to take you on your first date. If that's okay with you?"
He seemed delicate, different somehow, like he was frightened. Her eyes began to make their way up, from their hands, over his chest finally resting in his eyes. Those eyes, which could melt the heart of an ice queen.

"I love you, Adam." Her words escaped before she even realised what she was saying. It had the desired effect. Adam let out a huge sigh, his body visibly relaxing in front of her.

As he led her through the trees she came upon a small table, all set out with candles and silverware. Champagne rested in a bath of ice, rose petals scattered the table. It was perfect, everything she had ever imagined a perfect date could look like, he had done.
"So, are you hungry?" Adam pulled out one of the chairs for her to sit.
"Famished." All symptoms of her hangover vanished the minute she saw him.

The warm night air caressed her skin as Adam pushed her chair in and began to pour her a glass of champagne.
"You're not gonna propose, are you?" TJ cheekily grinned.
"God no, I love you but I'm not there yet, darling." Adam's confidence began to swarm back to him. His cocky little smile was making an appearance. "So this is how it is going to go, you are going to shut up, and I am going to speak," he announced.
"How romantic, you say the most wonderful things."
Adam placed his elbows onto the table and rested his hands under his chin, fixing TJ with an intently, serious glare.
"Proceed."

"Thank you, TJ, I was going to. Watching you walk away was the hardest thing I have ever done. I sat in the car for over two hours not knowing what the hell to do. You are the weirdest, most complicated woman I have ever known."

TJ let out a huff but Adam silenced her.

"I said I was talking."

TJ's toes curled at this dominant behaviour, not that she would usually allow it, but once in a while it would be acceptable. Especially if he looked this sexy.

"I started to think that maybe we couldn't work, maybe we were just too different. But then I got to thinking about the café and how hard it was in the beginning. How everyone said that a kid with no education wouldn't be able to run a business. But then Robert helped me and introduced me to Andrew and they helped me. They didn't tell me what to do, or how to do it, they guided me. That's when I decided to come home, I talked to Mum and Dad about how I felt. I didn't realise how shut off I had been until I saw my mother cry. Can you believe she cried because I had found love?" Adam stared down at the table as though ashamed. "I forget that I am her only child sometimes. I forgot that, the night you gave Mum the portrait. I didn't see how happy you had made Mum, you knew more about how she felt than I did. Anyway we had a long talk, about Brian and you, and we came to a decision."

"Is that the royal we, could you not come to the decision on your own?" A stab of worry shot through TJ, her stomach clenched in. Surely he would not do all this to leave her?

He reached out to hold her hand across the table, "I couldn't make this on my own because I cannot do it on my own. I need help if I want to have the life I can now see myself having, thanks to you."

Slowly he turned her hand over and stroked her wrists. "I can see it now."
TJ held her breath, "What can you see?"
"You, me, Bulldog and Bugsy all cuddled up in a house by the beach. I have seen a house, been thinking about it for ages, just never had the courage to do it. There is a guest house attached to the side, I figured that could be the dogs' apartment during the day. Mum and Maggie have agreed to pop in on the dogs during the day if we are not home and I also have the name of some excellent dog walkers."

TJ was in disbelief. "I don't want you to do all this for me, Adam." She suddenly began to freak out; making plans for the future was not her forte. It was scaring the living hell out of her. But for once, she didn't want to run. The feeling to hide away, forget all the trouble and just run away from it, was not there. Instead she began to see herself, walking the dogs along the beach. Lying in Adam's arms, watching TV.

Being a family.

Their conversation was interrupted by a gentleman bringing out food under large dome-covered silver dishes. The smell was divine and TJ's stomach growled in approval. A delicious, red steak lay underneath, nestled on a bed of lettuce with a rich, red sauce oozing over it. Her mouth began to drool at the sight of it. Potatoes and vegetables followed.

"This is amazing, Adam."

"Well, I have to admit it was a bit last minute, so we are kinda just having what Mum and Dad are having. Well, on posher plates of course!"

"Barbara, come away from that window this minute!" Derek chastised his wife, who was peeping round the wall to see through the window without being seen.

"I can't see what's going on. The food's gone out. I think they are eating."

"Well, at least someone is." Derek threw down his knife and fork. The loud clanking noise made Barbara turn around.

"Sorry. I just..."

"I know, dear, but you still have to eat." Derek once again picked up his cutlery, "...and keep your nose out. We raised a good boy, Babs; he knows what's good for him. And what is good for him is that girl."

Barbara nodded in agreement. She had never seen her boy like this before; they had spent so many years trying to get him to control his temper that he seemed to have suppressed all his other emotions as well. He saw girls, the odd night here and there. Barbara never got to meet most of them, not that she wanted to. Gold diggers, the lot of them. But TJ was different, TJ could stand toe to toe with him and meet him temper for temper. She had managed to draw out his feelings, make him realise he was missing something in his life.

That afternoon they had talked for hours, everything had been brought out into the open. It was very cathartic for all of them. When Adam had told her how much he loved TJ, not just how much, but the way he loved her. He had described all her idiosyncrasies, all the little details that made TJ... well, TJ.

It reminded her so much of Derek when they had first met. Barbara had been so insecure about the way she looked, about her place in society and most of all her loud, thunderous laugh. But Derek had told her that these were the things he had fallen in love with.

Here her son was doing the same thing; she felt a pressure on her heart, a desire to give her son everything he wanted. So happy that she even shed a tear for him. It was then he had told her about TJ's confession that she had never been on a date, and Barbara had immediately sprung into action.

Now she sat like a tiger waiting to pounce should anything go wrong, the only problem was putting them so far down the garden meant that she couldn't see what was happening. It was driving her nuts.

"That was delicious," announced TJ, wiping the remains of her plate with her finger, as she sucked the sauce from it. Adam watched her, listening to the little noises as she cleared the last drop. God, she was so sexy, and the thing that made it sexier, was that she had no idea what she was doing. No idea of the dirty, erotic images that were racing through his brain as she sucked the tips.

"Want to dance?" Adam stood and pressed buttons on his phone. A gentle song began to play all around her, the speakers hidden in amongst the branches. He reached out, inviting her to join him.

"You know this is where my father first asked my mum to marry him." He pressed his lips into TJ's soft hair, his arms snaking around her waist.

"What do you mean first?" TJ asked, distracted by the gossip.

Adam told her that they used to sneak in here when they were younger. It was one of the reasons Adam had bought the house for them. Derek had first proposed here only to be turned down. It took seven attempts before Barbara finally said yes. He never gave up, never made her feel bad about it, just kept believing that one day she would say yes.

"She was so worried about the whole marriage thing. Scared of getting hurt, scared of what people would say, scared of losing what they had. But Dad says that he knew, that he knew from the way she looked at him, that one day, when she was ready, she would say yes. So he kept asking, never waiting for a reply, just kept asking. Mum says she loved him for that, loved him for waiting."

He pulled her into him a little tighter, everything felt right. TJ in his arms, telling her all this. He hoped she would understand that he was telling her the same thing. That he would wait, until they were both ready, he would wait.

"Just how far can you see from that window?" TJ asked. Her eyes gazing into his with a desire she had not felt before. She needed him now, as though confirming and sealing their silent agreement.
"Are you kidding? My mum is probably watching us right now. She will be able to see us from there!"
"So, where can she NOT see us?" TJ's eyes met Adam's, her pupils dilated, her eyes wide.
Adam was powerless.

"I can't see them," Barbara declared in disgust. "They were dancing just a minute ago, I saw them."
"Maybe they have gone for a walk, Babs." Derek tried to calm his wife. "They do have a lot to talk about. I am pretty sure they won't want to have all their worries displayed out in front of the world."
"I am not the world! I am his mother and I have every right to know what is going on. I am going to see what's happening." Barbara stood to go out but Derek caught her arm.

"Babs, if things are not going well, you going off half cock down there might blow things altogether."

Barbara agreed with her husband and he loosened his grip, sliding his other hand around her waist.

"Of course, on the other hand, if things are going well, then they also won't want you storming down there." He hinted the suggestion.

"Fine," she spat out, "Oh, right." She realised what her husband was hinting at. "Oh God, did you have to say that!"

"I seem to remember us getting up to mischief the first time I proposed to you down there." Both hands now sneaked around his wife's waist as she let out a girly giggle.

"Yes, well, you were a bad boy. Adam is not!"

Derek released one arm and began to lead Barbara to the stairs. "I can be a bad boy again if you like!"

Chapter 24

TJ LAY IN ADAM'S ARMS, the only place she ever wanted to be. She felt cherished; everything just seemed in place when she was with him. There was no conflict, no surge of emotions wrestling within her, she felt at peace.

Casually, she traced a finger down his chest, his shirt still on but open. His muscles tightened as her hand stroked lower.
"If you carry on we are never going to leave this place." He cupped her face in his hand, stroking her hairline. "You are so beautiful, TJ."

Adam struggled to remember life before her. It was like he had lived life in a bubble, numb to everyone around him. Acting and reacting to whatever was in front of him and ignoring everything else.

He felt so different. Yes, he was still Adam Morgan, the businessman. But he was now so much more. TJ's warm hand rested on his stomach, it left a warm sensation wherever she touched. Everything would change now.

"Are you getting cold, baby?" Adam felt TJ quiver in his arms. Sitting up, he retrieved her top that had been thrown into the hedge.
"Adam." TJ sounded a little sleepy; she had been dozing off when the night chill had caused the light film of perspiration covering her skin to freeze. "Just so that you know, you will only have to ask me once. When the time is right, my answer will be yes."

Adam froze, rooted to the spot. Was she really saying what he thought she was saying? Was she really ready to be his? His throat became suddenly dry, words failing him.

He watched as TJ began to replace the missing clothing, her top strewn in a hedge, her trousers, screwed up on the floor.
"How is it that you always seem to remain dressed, whilst my clothes are all over the garden?" She raised her eyebrow quizzically at him. Adam just re-buttoned his shirt and jeans, smirking that annoyingly smug smile.

"So, how come your mum and dad used to sneak in here?" TJ asked after she slipped her shoes back on and now felt presentable again.
"I'll show you."

Helping TJ rise to her feet, his hand remained firmly clenched around hers as he led her through the trees and towards a small stone wall. TJ gazed out at the city, lit up in the distance. She could hear the gentle hum of traffic, not loud but just providing a white noise background. In amongst the haze, TJ could see Adam's apartment building, towering into the night sky. The top floor lights were indistinguishable from the stars now bustling for the spotlight.

Adam moved to stand behind her, wrapping his arms tightly round her. She sighed long and hard as his warmth enveloped her.

"The story goes like this. Mum was always conscious of going out with all my dad's friends. They were all great and loved her to pieces, but she always felt on edge, never relaxed around them. Dad took her to one side and asked her what was going on. She didn't know how to explain how she felt and so just told him she wanted a bit of time together. Just the two of them."

He nuzzled his nose into her hair, breathing in her strawberry shampoo. She relaxed back into him. He began to nibble her earlobe, playfully sucking it into his warm mouth.
"Stop that!" TJ insisted. "Story first!"
"Are you really turning me down, Tabby Cat?" His bottom lip jutted out.
"For gossip? - YES!"

Adam continued to tell her that his father had wracked his brains trying to find the perfect date. He had asked everyone for ideas but none seemed to be right.

"He just wanted everything to be perfect. He was walking to try and clear his head when he reached the road just down there."

TJ peered over the wall to see a little rickety bench; it sloped to the left and looked like it wouldn't take the weight of a fly. But she could imagine Derek, all those years ago, sitting there, staring out at the view of the city. During the day you would be able to see for miles. The dusty old road took you up a hill, giving the perfect vantage point.

"He thought that when Mum saw this, she might feel better, like she could belong. Because he knew she was worried about fitting in, even though she never told him. He climbed over the wall and found this little clearing."

"I bet your mum loved it, didn't she?" TJ asked, turning in his arms to watch him retell the story.

"I bought her the whole house and all the land, what do you think?"

Taking her by the shoulders, he spun her around and pointed to the trunk of one of the trees. Hardly visible was a heart carved into it,

D + B fell in love here,

had been scratched inside. TJ clutched her heart, it was so romantic, so innocent, she almost felt like crying.

"It was hard for them you see, not that Dad was posh or anything but Mum always felt he was above her. Like she would never fit in with his family. By all accounts Grandma was a total bitch. We don't see her much as I am sure you have guessed. She did her best to make Mum feel belittled at every opportunity, make her feel like staff."

"I cannot see your mum standing for that." TJ was taken aback.

"Mum was a different person back then, shy and timid. She took the abuse Dad's mother handed out and a small part of her believed it. She tried so hard to please his mother, read endless books on etiquette and correct behaviour, but nothing was ever enough.

"On top of all this stress, Dad kept proposing, wanting her to be his wife. But Mum knew that would cause so much trouble and he would end up having to choose between his family and her. There was no way she wanted to put him in that position, knowing full well he would choose her.

"Anyway, at the end of his tether, Dad had persuaded Mum to come up to their special place, he had a little picnic laid out ready for her. She used to wonder what would happen if the owners ever found out that the two lovers were squatting on their land. Dad had once again professed his love for her, once again asked her to be his. But this time he did not just dismiss her, he waited for a response. Apparently he said...

'Barbara, I don't want you to fit in with them. I want you to stand out, that is what I feel in love with. You. All of you. I want to be with you forever, whether you agree to marry me or not, woman, I am yours. Forever'."

Adam continued, "it was then he took out his penknife and began to carve into the tree. 'This will be here forever, just like my love for you will be here forever'. He held her hand against his heart and at that moment she finally understood. He would never let her go, never want her to change because he loved her as she was, not what she was trying to become."

"That was when she finally said yes." Adam finished his story; he stroked a stray hair from TJ's eyes. "I want love like that. With you."

"I don't want you to change for me though," TJ protested, her voice crackling, catching in her throat.

"You don't understand, I am not changing for you. I have pretended to be this person for so long, I forgot who I really was. That's what my dad wanted my mum to understand. To stop pretending to be something she wasn't. You reminded me of the person I used to be and I want to be that person again."

They both stood in silence their hearts beating in unison. Adam's eyes flashed to the side, pointing TJ to the tree next to his mother's and father's. TJ squinted her eyes to see, there was another carving,

Tabby Cat said YES to Adam here on...

The date had been left blank.

Adam reached into his pocket and pulled out a small penknife. Gently he wrapped TJ's fingers around it. Kissing her hand around the gift he smiled. "I love you," he whispered. "It's down to you now. Whenever you are ready."

He left TJ stunned, staring at the tree, the bare flesh of the tree exposed. Her head spinning with the story of his parents, their struggles, Adam's love. Could she do this? Could she cope with a full commitment?

Her fingertips stroked over the carving, then moved over to his parents' words.

If Barbara could do it, she was sure that she could.

Adam's silhouette lingered in the distance, waiting for her. Her heart settled at the sight, slowing from a heavy loud thumping, to a gentle quiet slow beat. That's what he did to her, that's the effect he had on her body.

She knew he would remain there, waiting for her.

Waiting until she was ready, just like his father.

She didn't want him to wait anymore.

Epilogue

IT TOOK A WHILE TO SORT EVERYTHING out. Everyone had pitched in to try and help Adam buy the beach house. Most of Adam's time had been taken up with helping the police with their investigation. They had a tech guy coming over to go through all their tills and records. It was going to cause a massive disruption but Adam didn't care. If he had to stand there and take cash for every order he would do. The rage he had initially felt had now turned into a sense of achievement. He felt good knowing that he could help in some way and help the poor girl's family get her justice.

Andrew, Adam's business manager, had been great whilst he was occupied with the police. Taking over all the purchasing, he had negotiated a quick sale and within two weeks Adam found himself the owner of a new house. Of course, he kept the apartment on for business; Andrew had been secretly pleased about that. He did not live in the city centre, so when meetings ran over late, it had been easier for him to just sleep over in the spare room, rather than drive all the way home only to come back after a few hours' sleep. His wife had long since come to accept this, it helped that Adam would often invite her up to stay when they had a weekend of work planned.

Andrew had even managed to purchase a large part of the beach in front of the house, which meant that they could fence it in and have a completely private area.

Malika had overseen Bulldog's transition. From purchasing all his bedding, food and toys to designing the side apartment that he would be spending the days in when Adam was working.
He seemed to sense that something was going on, Adam was visiting a lot more than usual. Also, he was having to do courses with some strange-smelling woman who kept trying to make him sit on the same spot, or walk next to her. Why would he want to walk next to her when his best friend was over the other side? Maggie had nearly had a heart attack, when Adam had taken her for a visit.

"That's not a bloody dog, it's a bear. What the hell are you expecting me to do with that?" But Bulldog had soon won her round, placing his overly large head into her hand and turning his head so she could scratch his ear. Maggie melted, huge puppy dog eyes locked on hers and she was sold. "I suppose it would be nice to have a walk along the beach every day," she conceded.

In just three weeks, Adam had gone from thinking about buying the place, to hiring people to move all his stuff. He sighed loudly at the pitiful handful of boxes that contained his life. Was it possible that in all the time he had lived in this apartment, he had only collated five boxes of possessions? He had decided to leave most of his things here because he had never really picked any of it out. A decorator had come in and, with his mother, they had furnished the place. He wanted his new home to be different, to be his own creation. Barbara had tried to offer her services, advising him of where to place furniture but he was having none of it. This was his, and hopefully one day, TJ's.

Grabbing the last of his clothes, he headed down to the lobby. The doorman offered him a hearty handshake and Adam felt a lump develop in his throat as he left the building. It was ridiculous, he was not leaving altogether. He would be in town as much as at home.

Home.

An excited feeling flooded him, a home. Not just a place or apartment. He was going home.

TJ tapped her fingernails on her mobile phone impatiently. Adam was due to collect her at any moment to take her to see the new house. He was collecting things from his apartment then heading over to hers. Her mum and dad had already picked Bugsy up to allow her a bit of time to see the place. They had developed quite a bond with the ugly mutt and whenever she said their names, Bugsy would get excited and wag his little tail, dashing off to drag his blanket over to the door. Stopovers at her parents' had started to become a regular thing. She suspected her dad had a soft spot for him.

Her phone suddenly buzzed, making her jump. Her heart leapt up into her throat.

Adam was outside.

"Holy crap, Adam." The house was all on one level, completely open plan. It was the most beautiful place she had ever seen. No furniture cluttered the amazing space. Adam had decided not to invest in anything until Bulldog had settled in.
Just in case.

A wall of windows framed the ocean. The doors led straight onto a little decking area; there was nothing between them and the ocean but the beach. TJ stood mesmerised by the sound of the waves gentle lapping, the soundtrack to serenity.
"You like it?" Adam quizzed. TJ was a hard woman to read. "I guess you wish you had your camera." From behind a cardboard box he pulled out a case. "For when you're here."

TJ slowly opened the case to reveal a Nikon D4 Camera. Her mouth dropped open; speechless she ran her fingers over the case, the lenses nestled in neat rows.
"I talked to Suzy; she said this was a camera that you always wanted. Did I do well?"

His smug grin could not be hidden. He knew she loved it. Suzy had gone into overdrive talking to all the tutors for their opinions on what to buy. When she had contacted Adam, her words had been, "This is gonna cost you, Adam, but she will love it."
"In that case, whatever it costs will be worth it."

Adam watched TJ giddily prance around the apartment, listing all the features the camera had. All the different lenses and functions. He did not understand a word of what she was saying, but he was caught up in her excitement as she cradled the camera like a child.

She was ultimately drawn to the ocean. The night beginning to draw in, the sea had a purple tinge to it. The sun disappearing in a haze of chalky light, the moon spreading a silver sparkle across all it saw.
"I have a confession to make." Adam followed her out to the decking. "I knew you were watching me. That night on the balcony. I saw you."
"What?" TJ's humiliation came flooding back to her. "You saw me?"

"Not taking pictures, I had no idea you'd done that till the next morning. But yes, you, I did see."

"So why did you carry on?" TJ did not understand.

"I heard a noise, turned and saw you sliding down the wall outside. I dunno, I guess I thought I'd punish you for being nosey. I was cross at first. But then, when I saw the pictures. I saw how beautiful they were. How you had seen the events of that night."

TJ chortled, "There wasn't exactly a lot to interpret." Her skin began to prickle at the thought of Adam with another woman, touching another woman. Why was he talking about this now?

"I don't even remember her name; she was just a means to an end. But knowing you were out there kinda turned me on. I sent her home by the way. We went into the bedroom and I asked her to leave. She slapped me, called me every name under the sun and then left. I thought to myself you could stay out there as punishment. I didn't think you would stay there all night, I guess you fell asleep."

TJ guessed she deserved that, she had not felt brilliant about it herself. "I am sorry, Adam, I wasn't..."

Adam shook his head. "No, listen. When I came out the next morning and saw you still there, I understood. You weren't being nosey. The fact that you stayed outside showed that you respected my privacy and didn't invade my space. Even though I had chucked her out, you didn't know that and hadn't come back. I really respected you for that. I made you a coffee and brought it out to you. You were slumped down and looked so uncomfortable. I leant down and whispered your name to wake you. But you just muttered my name back, then all these erotic noises began."

Adam could picture her, her chest heaving, her succulent lips murmuring his name. It had taken all his strength not to take her there and then.
"You know I was dreaming about you, don't you?" TJ confessed. Adam just showed that smug, confident smile.
"What was I doing to you, Tabby Cat? Did you replace that woman with yourself?"

TJ's face glowered, embarrassment heating her face, burning it like the mid-day sun.
"Tell me, what was I doing?" Adam took her hand and led her back into the house. "Was I doing this?" Without warning Adam threw her against the wall, re-enacting the amazing photographs that TJ had taken that night. "Tell me, TJ," Adam whispered against her neck as his whole body crushed her against the wall, his lips devouring her neck leaving TJ panting, unable to breathe. "Was I doing this?" His hand slid down and grasped TJ's knee, hoisting her leg up to his waist.
TJ cried out in agreement, "Yes. Yes, Adam."

Needing no more encouragement, he yanked her jeans from her, returning to the same position the second she was free of them. Ripping her underwear to the side he began to explore, his head still adoring her neck, her chest.

"I need you," she managed to pant. Her hands lowered to undo his buttons and zip. He pulled back a little; just enough to watch her hungry eyes as she used her feet to slide the trousers down. "NOW."

Adam's sharp intake of breath sent waves of pleasure coursing through TJ's body. Just the thought of what he was about to do had her contracting to control the release.

"We're gonna be happy, TJ."

"Forever," TJ gasped as pleasure began to rip through her.

"Then come for me, Tabby Cat, let me feel you."

TJ could hold out no more, she cried out as her body had her literally climbing further up the wall, Adam's hands holding her down. She felt his lips against her ear, his hot breath flowing down her neck.

"Tell me anything, Tabby Cat, any fantasy, any desire. I WILL make them happen."

TJ opened her eyes long enough to see Adam's eyes turn almost black. Desire raging through him, he had been holding back, waiting for her to join him. With her hand's guidance, he was in her, consuming her, filling her life.

Her eyes closed once more as she allowed Adam to take control.

Allowed him to let go.

The story continues in Bittersweet Serenade ...

Thank you for taking the time to read my books, if you liked this story please read on for excerpts of other books in The Coffee Café Series.

If you would like more information on any of my books please take a look at my website www.crmcbride.co.uk where you can subscribe to receive up to date information on any of my books and be the first to know release dates and read any teasers.

You can follow me on Twitter or on Facebook all links are on my website.

Thank you

Bittersweet Serenade

FRANK BENTON HAS THREE MURDERED girls and as yet no suspects. Adam Morgan, the owner of The Coffee Café had provided some assistance but he needs to get more.

An old friend, Jamie, is going to help go through all the computer files, cameras and technical mumbo jumbo to see what he can find. Frank does not hold out much hope. Killers like this, men and women, often vanish into the night, uncaught, and unpunished.

But Frank is not ready to give up yet, as his sister always used to say, "there is always a paper trail," or in this case a digital trail.

Whoever did these killings, Frank was determined to find them. Unfortunately to find more evidence, it was inevitable that there would have to be more killings.

The figure stood in the doorway, hidden from sight amongst the shadows.

It was her!

After all these years of searching, she had suddenly turned up. Right in front of him, just sitting there, having a cup of coffee. Her laughter hummed through the glass window. At last he could have his revenge. She was going to feel his pain, feel everything he had felt.

His breath was laboured as he tried to control his need. Now was not the right time. She would wait. He had other matters to deal with first. All this time planning, making arrangements and now everything was happening.

Happening all at once.

Taking one last long look, he finally dragged himself away from the window. Things would have to be stepped up, that was all. He no longer had to watch, no longer had to hide and follow in secret.

Tomorrow.

Just one more night and all his dreams would be fulfilled.

She would pay and he would be there to make her pay.

He cowered, diving into an alley as several people walked by laughing and joking. They did not notice him, no one ever noticed him.

Even in all the carnage of what was about to happen, no one would notice him. They would cry and hold each other. They would wonder how anyone could do something so vile.

Still no one would notice him.

Even when the last heart stopped beating.

No one would notice him.

Bitter Reflections by C.R. McBride

SARA ROLLED HER EYES, REGRETTING that she had picked up the damn phone, this was not going to help her mood. Jamie worked at her company, Saltec; it sold and installed computer equipment to companies all over the world. He was one of the company 'geeks', with scruffy black hair and an endless supply of black faded t-shirts, he had been persistently trying to get Sara to go out with him since she asked him for help three months ago.

Not many people ventured into the 'geeks' domain and if they did they never went back again. It wasn't that they were unpleasant,   they were all really intelligent people but their social skills were a bit, well lacking, they seemed to speak a whole different language to most people but expected everyone to automatically know what they were on about. If only she'd known that a missing order could cause so much hassle, she wouldn't have bothered chasing it, having to ask him to help her find it, and would have just re-entered it into the system manually.

"Sara! Are you there?" Jamie asked down the line after Sara had not replied, She sighed, unable to keep the frustrated tone from her voice.

"Yes, I'm here, it's just that I am rather busy, Jamie, and to be honest not the best company at the moment."

It was so hard to not upset his feelings but Jamie was about twelve years old, well OK, not twelve but there was no way that he was older than twenty three and with Sara approaching her thirty-fifth birthday there was no way that her sex life had become so depressing that she was going to scrape the bottom of the barrel by becoming a cougar.

"You are mental!" her friend Jo had screeched at her when she had told her about Jamie's advances. "You should totally go for it, it's not like you're getting any from anyone else!"

"Shut up! He's a child; there's no way on earth I am going out with a child, he probably plays computer games all day!" Sara complained.

"You have had no decent man in your life since you left 'The Bastard', Sara, and let's be honest, with the hours you work you hardly fit time in to see me let alone start a relationship!" It was true, Jo was right, she just had no free time whatsoever at the moment, lonely didn't begin to describe how she felt and as for her sex life, it was non-existent. Other than a few thrills from the romance novels that Jo lent her, she had given up on men; Jo, however, moved freely from one guy to the next, never really looking for anything permanent, just someone to have fun with. Sara could never be like that, she had tried it once with a bloke from the coffee shop, Troy, what a disaster. Sara was not fun like Jo, she had been nervous on the date and not interested in him at

all, the night had been a total disaster and after a very weak attempt of seduction on his part and some fumbling Sara had sent him packing and decided quick flings were not for her! Why couldn't she just meet someone like the men out of her books, someone who understood her, who loved her and seduced her passionately but there were no men like that in real life!

"Is he good looking, Sara? If so, you are an idiot for not going for it," Jo insisted.

Mmm, that had been a good question, the truth was she had never really looked at Jamie that way before, she didn't even know his full name. But even still, he was so much younger than her and she was not getting into that, no way.

"Sara, are you still there?" the voice continued.

"Oh God, sorry, Jamie, I went off in a daydream then, yeah I'm fine, just a bit of bad news that's all. Look I really appreciate the offer but Jamie, I just want to be alone tonight."

There was a long pause before he asked almost in a whisper:

"Does that mean that there may be a night when you don't want to be alone?"

Sara couldn't help herself and let out a little giggle, you've gotta love the persistence and eternal hope of youth. She said goodnight and put down the phone, not feeling half as bad as she did before she had picked it up.

Absolute Resolve

NICK SHRANK UNDER THE BLANKETS as Melissa threw the curtains back, allowing the blinding sun to stream into the room. "For fuck's sake, Melissa!"

"Oh well, that's nice talk on a gloriously beautiful summer morning," she sang out. Nick just grunted and tried to disappear further down the bed. "Don't even start with that, Nick," she scolded, ripping the duvet off the bed. "You have interviews all day, get up, get dressed and get out there!" The dirty look that Nick threw her said everything he needed to say, he was NOT a morning person and absolutely hated the way Melissa was all bright eyed and bushy tailed the minute her alarm went off.

"Coffee," he moaned.

"You don't even drink coffee, Nick, now get up!"

"Maybe I need to start drinking it if you are gonna drag my arse out of bed at this time every morning!"

"Stop being a baby."

"Stop treating me like a baby."

"Stop acting like a baby then."

"Stop....stop... oh I can't be arsed."

Melissa shook her head as Nick shuffled off into the bathroom, she loved him so much. Nick had been a timid young man when his mother had introduced them. Through her work in the theatres Nick's mother had a lot of contacts among agents and producers, even many actors but never told Nick that and never used them. Her Nick needed to make it on his own and he would not thank her for trying to help him. When she found out that Melissa had left her old agency firm she had called her and asked if she would be interested in calling round for dinner. Melissa had nothing else planned so had agreed. Nick had been a gangly-looking man back then. He had finished university and had a few jobs but felt like writing was his passion. Up until that point he had only written as a hobby, but as soon as Melissa read his story she knew what his mother had been up to. The way Nick's writing captured her heart was unique, of course he refused to believe that he was anywhere near good enough to be published but Melissa and his mother had persisted. It had taken two months to persuade him to let anyone else read it, then longer to get him to let them try to get it published. Now here they were an instant hit, Melissa had hoped that having just celebrated his twenty sixth birthday, Nick might have grown up more and stood up to the pressure of a public life. That, however, was not proving to be the case and he just shrunk away from cameras and fans. Never mind, he was talented and Melissa was going to make sure that he was protected and she would not allow him to be bullied into doing things he did not want to do, baby steps with Nick.

Nick looked at his reflection as he stepped out of the shower, yes he was tall and had dark hair and true, since he had joined the local gym his body was beginning to take on shape, but really he was no oil painting in his opinion. What did all these girls see in him? They would scream at him, hand him phone numbers and now they were sending him their knickers! It was surreal, beyond weird and quite scary sometimes. He never had women chasing him before he was famous, they would call him 'sweet' or 'such a good friend'. Never had they wanted to date him, so what was so different now? Melissa yelling through the door shook him from his thoughts; he dried himself and went to get dressed.

"Please tell me you are not planning on wearing that thing!" Melissa gasped as Nick joined her for breakfast.

"What's wrong with it?" Nick stood looking down at his favourite jumper; he was doing a radio interview, why did he have to get dressed up?

"You look like you are going fishing, Nick! For goodness sake! Get it off!"

Nick pouted. "I love this jumper."

"OFF!"

"Fine." Nick stripped it off and sat down to breakfast bare-chested, grinning. "Happy now?"

Melissa tried in vain to hide her amusement. "Funny," she said sarcastically, "Drink your tea."

"Yes, agent mummy."

"Carry on and I will call your mother and tell her what a sulky child you are being," she threatened.

"OK, OK." He held his hands up in surrender, "So what's on the menu today?"

Melissa ran through the day's interviews and events with him. "A few magazine interviews, they will be basic girly questions, what's your favourite colour? Favourite film? Etc. etc. Usual stuff, then there's that one." She pointed to a book magazine, "That one wants to talk to you about which books influenced you as a child and what you are reading now!" Reading now! Were they kidding? When did he have time to read?

"What are you reading?" he asked Melissa as he shoved half a slice of buttered toast into his mouth.

"Erotica!" she smirked. "Would you like the title and author?"

"Ha ha, funny! Well, if you're not going to help me?"

"Look, just go online and look to see if there are any books you fancy and I'll have them brought up then you can say you've just started them." She continued down the list, "Last of the day is the radio interview with Dave Glinson." Nick groaned, Dave Glinson was an 'all about the gossip who needed the truth when you could make it up' sort of person.

"Why do I have to do an interview with him? He does movie stars and singers, why would he want to interview a first time author?"

Melissa rolled her eyes, "Do you realise how popular your book is becoming? Everyone is talking about it; authors are rapidly becoming the new rock stars!" She noticed the worry on his face. "Don't worry, I will get a list of questions that he wants to ask beforehand and tell him personal life is a no go area, OK!" She ruffled his hair affectionately. "Come on, sausage, let's get you into something more appropriate that doesn't make you look like you are going tuna fishing!"

"So who is your favourite singer?" The young girl asked, gazing up at him, for four hours he had answered the same questions, tried to be polite, tried to be honest but really none of this was important. Who cared how he kept in shape? Whether he was on a diet, or worst still was, "Do you have a girlfriend at the moment?" He just wanted to talk about his book, what inspired him to write the story, where the ideas came from but no one was interested. Even the interview with the book magazine was dull. He had started to talk about his childhood books but they had deviated, asking him whether he thought sex was appropriate in young adult reads! What sort of discussion was that to have? There was no sex in his book, well a small bit but nothing graphic or explicit, so why were they asking him this? By the time they got around to his actual story they had run out of time, then asked if they could get some pictures and would he mind undoing his shirt – talk about hypocritical.

"Mr Mill-Thorpe?"

"Oh sorry, I don't really get time to listen to music much, I do like a lot of songs but don't really follow anyone in particular." That should please Melissa, a non-committal answer.

"Could you name any songs then?" she continued.

Damn. "Well, I grew up in the theatre, so a lot of the songs I really love are from musicals and plays." The girl looked at him blankly so he just ran off a few pop songs that he had heard in the car on the way over, now was the interview he was dreading the most, the radio interview with the repulsive Dave Glinson.

"You need to eat something, Nick," Melissa all but pleaded with him, "It will be OK, I promise." Nick nodded gloomily; they were in a tiny restaurant that Melissa had found round the back of the radio station. It matched his mood perfectly; the mood lighting left the room dark so no one could see any distance, therefore removing the risk of being spotted. Dark shadows bounced off the walls, making everyone unrecognisable. He picked at the lasagne in front of him, his stomach churning over and over again, he just didn't have the nerve to do this. Melissa kept telling him that things would die down and that it wouldn't be this bad all the time but the opposite was happening, the interest in him was just growing and it was very uncomfortable.

"I need a drink," he announced.

"I don't think that's a good idea, do you?"

"Yes, as a matter of fact I do, I need to take the edge off my nerves." He ordered a beer and drank the whole bottle down in one. This was not good, Melissa watched as he ordered another, maybe she should cancel the interview. No, that would be no good, Dave would just make up a load of rubbish to get back at them, no, she had to sort him out as best she could and get him into that studio.

"Nick. Can I call you Nick?"

"Sure, that is my name after all."

"It's just with a name like Nicholas Mill-Thorpe, I feel like I should call you sir!" A rumble of laughter rippled round the studio.

"Nick is fine."

"So, forgive me if I move further round the table, beer and lasagne for lunch I am guessing, from the smell of garlic! Do you always drink through the day, Nick?" Melissa let out a long exasperated sigh; Nick scrunched his hands into a ball. Calm and polite, that's what Melissa always told him, calm and polite.

"Only when I am celebrating being on a show as huge and popular as yours." Dave smirked at Nick's rebound.

"Greasing all the right poles, eh Nick? OK, we are going to play another song and then get straight back to Nick to ask him about his long term relationship with Tanya and why he broke her heart! Back in two."

Nick looked at Melissa, panic strewn across his face. Melissa was in a furious argument with one of the show's producers. She was frantically waving the list of pre-set questions in his face. "Shit," he cursed into his hand as he ran it across his chin, this was gonna be hell.

"Nick, slow down," Melissa called out as Nick practically ran from the taxi into the hotel lobby. "Nick, listen to me!" She caught the lift doors and slid in next to him.

"What the fuck was that? Who the hell is Tanya?"

Melissa took a breath. "It seems some girl who went to school with you sold her story to the press, told them you dated and that you broke her heart!"

"How?" Nick asked quietly.

"What?"

"How did I supposedly break her heart?"

Melissa paused looking at the seriousness of his face. "Slept with her friend," she muttered.

Nick rubbed his temples with both hands, "Well, that's just fucking great isn't it!"

"It's not that bad, look that's it now for this week, have an early night and..."

"And what, Melissa? Everything will be alright in the morning, bollocks," he shouted, making her retreat to the back of the lift. They rode the rest of the floors in silence; Melissa frantically tried to think of something to say but failed. Nick was a good kid; he prided himself on his manners and reputation. In one fell swoop this vicious girl had taken that away from him. Melissa made a note to herself that she would sue that cow and make her pay for this. "I know it's not you, Melissa," Nick practically whispered as they reached his door, but still he couldn't look at her.

"I will sort it; I promise I will not let anything like this happen again, I will sort everything from now on." She tried to kiss him on his forehead, which was quite a feat for a little woman like her. Nick smiled as she struggled, and taking pity on her, leaned down allowing her to complete the tender, affectionate gesture. His smile broadened a little and he opened his door but very quickly faltered at the sight of a naked girl lying across his bed. He turned to look at Melissa, taking her hand he led her to the edge of the bed. The girl stared at Nick, speechless at finally realising her dream to sleep with Nick Mill-Thorpe.

"You're in luck," he said sarcastically. Then pointed to the girl, his eyes never leaving Melissa's, "Sort that!" Then he turned and slammed the door behind him, leaving Melissa with tears pouring down her cheeks and a very confused naked girl who was about to feel Melissa's wrath.

Thank you for taking the time to read my books, if you liked this story please read on for excerpts of other books in The Coffee Café Series, Bitter Reflections and Distinct Desire.

If you would like more information on any of my books please take a look at my website www.crmcbride.co.uk where you can subscribe to receive up to date information on any of my books and be the first to know release dates and read any teasers.

You can also follow me on Twitter or on Facebook all links are on my website.

Thank you

Acknowledgments

Thanks as always to Caroline Easton and Julia Gibbs for reading through for me and polishing up. xxx

To my big sister, Andrea, for spending her time in between working and encouraging me all the way. Love ya.

Other Titles by C.R McBride

Bitter Reflections
Part 1 of The Coffee Café Series

Absolute Resolve

Part 2 of The Coffee Café

Made in the USA
Charleston, SC
03 February 2016